ENDGAME

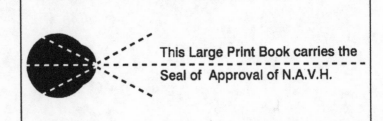

A NAMELESS DETECTIVE NOVEL

ENDGAME

BILL PRONZINI

THORNDIKE PRESS
A part of Gale, a Cengage Company

A Cengage Company

Farmington Hills, Mich • San Francisco • New York • Waterville, Maine
Meriden, Conn • Mason, Ohio • Chicago

Copyright © 2017 by the Pronzini-Muller Family Trust.
Thorndike Press, a part of Gale, a Cengage Company.

ALL RIGHTS RESERVED
This is a work of fiction. All of the characters, organizations, and events portrayed in this novel are either products of the author's imagination or are used fictitiously.
Thorndike Press® Large Print Mystery.
The text of this Large Print edition is unabridged.
Other aspects of the book may vary from the original edition.
Set in 16 pt. Plantin.

LIBRARY OF CONGRESS CIP DATA ON FILE.
CATALOGUING IN PUBLICATION FOR THIS BOOK
IS AVAILABLE FROM THE LIBRARY OF CONGRESS
ISBN-13: 978-1-4328-4389-2 (hardcover)

Published in 2018 by arrangement with Macmillan Publishing Group, LLC/Tor/Forge

Printed in Mexico
1 2 3 4 5 6 7 22 21 20 19 18

For Marcia

Prologue

The two cases came into the agency within half an hour of each other on a Wednesday afternoon in May.

Both had their unusual aspects, though they seemed straightforward enough as far as our services went. Had there only been the Cahill matter, Tamara would have assigned Jake Runyon to it. But because the Dennison job came in first and required a four-hundred-plus-mile round-trip drive into the Sierras, the first leg with a female passenger, Runyon was given that one; and because Alex Chavez and both of our part-time operatives were out on field assignments and I happened to be in the office with nothing but routine to occupy my time, I took James Cahill's call and agreed to interview him.

If Runyon or Chavez or anybody else had handled the Cahill investigation, its ultimate outcome might have been different. One thing for sure: it would not have worked out in the same way, with the same consequences, if I hadn't been the one to take it on.

Life can be a real bitch sometimes.

1

Shelter Hills Estates was one of those modern suburban housing developments that proliferate in just about every town large and small in the Greater Bay Area, elsewhere in California, and no doubt throughout the entire country. Cookie-cutter homes for what's left of the American middle class. This one, in Walnut Creek, was the upscale variety: quarter-acre lots containing large two-story homes built of stucco, redwood, and glass in an odd architectural blend of ranch and town house. They appeared to come in two sizes, three- and four-bedroom; if there were any other differences in their construction, they weren't apparent to me. The only way you could tell them apart was by their owners' preferences for color schemes, landscaping, and external alterations and embellishments.

James Cahill's residence was on a winding

street saddled with the kind of cutesy name developers are fond of, Sweet William Drive. There was nothing particularly distinctive about the place. Its color scheme, which may have been the original, because there were others like it in the development, was a sort of creamy tan with medium brown trim. The front and side yards were low maintenance, mostly ornamental grasses and small plants in a sea of redwood chips — maybe in deference to the drought, maybe not. Cahill's south-side neighbor was drought conscious, at least, judging from the crusty brown remnants of what had once been a lawn. A white BMW sedan was parked in the driveway in front of a wide attached garage, a "2.5 garage" in Realtors' parlance. Meaning, I suppose, that there's room inside for two full-sized vehicles plus motorcycles, scooters, bicycles, or whatever else you might want to stuff into the .5 section.

It was a couple of minutes shy of noon when I pulled up in front. I don't usually agree to conduct a preliminary interview at a prospective client's home, but Cahill had said it was important that I come here for pertinent reasons and offered to pay the expense whether I accepted his case or not. I'd had a similar offer not long ago, from a man in Atherton, and the result had been bizarre and disturbing. From what Cahill had told me on the phone, his problem was more or less conventional — a missing wife.

The house was outfitted with an ADT wireless security system, as testified to by a panel with a sticker on it next to the door. Good for Cahill; home break-ins were all too common in neighborhoods like this. There was also a mail slot in the door, something you don't often see in modern development homes.

My first impression when Cahill opened the door was of a man under extreme strain and struggling to cope. Nervous tic at one corner of a broad mouth, dark shadows under green eyes with blood-flecked whites, a moist handshake. He looked to be in his mid-thirties and was losing what was left of his dark brown hair. There was plenty of hair on his body, though; curls and tufts of it showed through the open collar of his blue dress shirt.

He didn't seem to mind the fact that I was old enough to be his father and then some; if anything, it seemed to reassure him. Age translates to wisdom in some people's view. If only that were true in my case, I thought wryly. I've learned some things over the years, but the older I get, the more I realize just how much I don't know or understand and never will. Wise? Sometimes I feel like I ought to be wearing a dunce cap.

"Thank you for coming," he said. His voice, like the rest of him, was twitchy. "I really appreciate it. We can talk in the living room, okay?" As if asking for my approval in his own home. "The family room's a little messy. I'm not much of a housekeeper."

"Wherever you prefer, Mr. Cahill."

"The living room, then. This way."

The living room had hardly been lived in at all. That was the feeling you got walking into it — big, neat, well furnished, and neglected. Nothing out of place, nothing to alleviate the unblemished formality except a faint coating of dust on lampshades and tables.

Cahill saw me glancing around and correctly interpreted what I was thinking. "Alice and I don't use this room much. The family room, her office, mine . . . it's a big house. We don't have any kids. Planned on having a couple, that's one reason we bought the place, but . . . ah, Christ, I'm running off at the mouth. I'm sorry."

"No need to apologize."

"It's just that I'm nervous as hell. Hardly slept at all last night, trying to make up my mind what to do. I couldn't have gone to work today if my life depended on it." He was regional sales director for a company that manufactured small household appliances, he'd told me on the phone. "Well . . . please, sit wherever you like."

He went to perch on a semi-ugly upholstered chair — autumn leaves on a pale yellow background. I sat on its mate, facing him across a glass-topped table with an arrangement of chrome bars as its base. Definitely not a room designed for either comfort or socializing. More like the kind of artificial setup you find in furniture showroom displays.

"You said on the phone that your wife has been missing for . . . a week, was it?"

"That's right. Seven days. I'm worried sick about her."

"And that you filed a missing-person report with the police."

"For all the good it's done. They think I did something to her. That's what just about everybody thinks — her sister, her brother-in-law, most of the neighbors. . . . But I didn't; I swear I didn't."

"What makes them all think you did?"

"Because in their minds I'm the only person who had cause."

"I don't understand. She could have left of her own free will, for one reason or another, couldn't she?"

"That's just it. No. No, she couldn't. Couldn't have left at all unless somebody took her out, and to do that they'd have had to knock her unconscious or . . . worse."

"I still don't understand —"

"Alice is agoraphobic," Cahill said. "She hasn't been out of this house in over four years. Not once for as much as five seconds. She couldn't even step onto the front porch without having a panic attack."

Well, that was something new in my experience. Plenty of people have phobias — I'm somewhat acrophobic myself — but I'd never professionally encountered a severe anxiety disorder. "You didn't say anything about this when we spoke earlier."

"No, I . . . no. I'm sorry, I thought it might . . . oh God, I don't know what I thought. I'm such a wreck I can't think straight." He hopped to his feet so abruptly he might have been goosed into it. "You don't mind if I have a drink, do you? I don't usually drink this early in the day, or much at all, but I can really use one right now."

Despite his disclaimer, he'd already had at least one before I got there; I'd smelled the liquor on his breath when we shook hands. "No, I don't mind," I said, and I didn't as long as he stayed reasonably sober. "Better make it light, though."

"Right. I will. You want one?"

"No thanks."

He went out in long, jerky strides. The house was so still I could hear him bartending in whatever other room he'd gone into. Pretty soon he came back with a tumbler half-full of amber liquid and rattling ice cubes. The color of the scotch or bourbon was such that I figured he'd kept his promise to make the drink light. Small point in his favor. He resumed his perch, seemed about to take a long swallow, changed his mind, and made it a sip instead.

"How long have you lived here, Mr. Cahill?"

"How long? Five and a half, almost six years."

"So your wife hasn't always been agoraphobic."

"No. No, it was the goddamn . . . excuse me, the accident that did it."

"What sort of accident?"

"She was driving home from visiting a friend in Danville one night, late. It was raining and . . . I don't know, she braked too hard or something; her SUV went into a skid through an intersection and broadsided a smaller car. Injured the driver, killed the passenger. Alice wasn't hurt, thank God, just shaken up."

"Was she impaired in any way that night?"

"You mean had she been drinking? No. Nothing like that. It was just one of those things that happen . . . the rain, the slippery pavement, poor visibility. But being responsible for killing someone tore her up, affected her mind. She wouldn't drive after that, wouldn't even get into a car. Then things just got progressively worse."

"You sought treatment for her?"

Cahill took another, larger sip before answering. "Three sessions with a specialist in anxiety disorders before she refused to leave the house at all. Didn't do any good. Do you know anything about agoraphobia?"

"Just the basics."

"Well, Alice's is about as bad as it gets. Not only intense fear of open spaces, but fear of death, fear of strangers — the only people she'll deal with on a regular basis are me, her sister Kendra, Kendra's husband, and her best friend from college, Fran Woodward. She's afraid of everything, including the panic attacks. When she has one of those she —" He broke off, shaking his head, and drained the tumbler. "You have no idea what it's like living with a person with that sort of disorder."

"No, I don't."

16

"Frustrating, frightening, maddening. It's like I'm trapped in here with her a lot of the time. I mean we have no social life except for the three people I mentioned. All the friends we had before drifted out of my life as well as hers. Being here alone with her is like walking on eggshells. A lot of the time she's depressed, withdrawn. Other times she flies off the handle for no reason. Calm one minute, her old self or close to it, the next something sets her off and she starts shaking, yelling . . . saying crazy paranoid things."

"What sort of paranoid things?"

"That I hate her, wish she was dead, might decide to kill her someday. She said something to Kendra about it and Kendra told the cops — the main reason they think I did away with her."

"How often do those kinds of flare-ups happen?"

"Not often. Usually when she forgets to take her meds."

"In the presence of others or just you?"

"Mostly just me. When she's like that she lashes out, nearly brained me with a lamp once when I tried to calm her down. All I did was embrace her, but in her panic she thought I was trying to strangle her." Cahill brooded into his empty glass. "It's all just a . . . nightmare fantasy with her. I wouldn't hurt her. I still love her, in spite of everything. My God, if I didn't I'd have divorced her long ago. But who'd take care of her if I did? She's not equipped to live alone with only occasional supervision."

"What does she do with her time? Read? Watch TV?"

"Writes, mostly."

"Writes?"

"Books. Romance novels. She's always loved reading that kind of stuff. She wrote one before the accident, but it wasn't until afterward, closed up in here, that she really got into it. Creates worlds she can control and escape into, that's what she says. If she didn't have that . . ."

"Have any of her books been published?"

"Oh, yes. About a dozen."

"Under her own name?"

"Hers and a pseudonym, Jennifer West. All for a paperback and e-book publisher in New York. She's making good money now, building a name for herself, getting positive feedback from fans. But there's one nut case in S.F. who's been harassing her recently."

"Harassing her how?"

"With a series of e-mails. Claims Alice plagiarized a cheap self-published novel of hers."

"Did the woman threaten her?"

"To smear her with her publisher unless Alice paid her off. Attempted extortion, plain and simple."

"How did your wife handle the situation?"

"Well . . . she tried to make it go away by reasoning with the woman and, when that didn't work, just ignored her. She printed out the e-mails; I can show them to you."

"You think this woman might be responsible for your wife's disappearance?"

"I don't know what to think. But if she showed up here, Alice would never have let her in the house."

I said, "Tell me about the day your wife disappeared. When did you last see her?"

"Just before I left for work, about eight-thirty."

"What was her state of mind then?"

"Agitated. I don't know why; she wouldn't say. But she'd run out of Valium and was low on Paxil, the drugs she takes for anxiety and panic attacks and depression."

"Did you talk to her during that day? Text or e-mail her?"

"No. I don't, usually — she doesn't like to be interrupted while she's writing."

"What time did you get home that evening?"

"A little after six, as usual. I knew right

19

away something was wrong because the security system was off."

"Your wife always kept it armed when she was here by herself?"

"Always."

"Would she turn it off for anyone other than the three you mentioned?"

"Only if it was absolutely necessary," Cahill said, "like for a delivery of some kind or a repairman. She couldn't deal with anyone but the four of us for more than a few minutes at a time, not if she was alone in the house."

"Who else knows the security code?"

"Just Alice and me. She didn't want anyone else to have it."

"Were there any signs of a disturbance, anything out of place?"

"No. Alice was just . . . gone."

"All the doors and windows secure?"

"Except the kitchen door to the garage. She kept that locked, too, but I found it unlocked. That must be how she was . . . taken away."

"Anything missing? Clothing, jewelry, valuables?"

"Nothing except her laptop. I looked through the bedroom closet, her bureau drawers, the bathroom. All her meds are still in the cabinet. The new supply of Valium

Kendra dropped off was still on the kitchen counter, unopened. Alice must have calmed down without needing to take one."

"Dropped off that day?"

"Around ten-thirty. Kendra picked them up at the pharmacy. Her husband, Paul Nesbitt, is Alice's doctor. She stayed about half an hour, and Alice was fine when she left."

"Did the best friend have any contact with her that day?"

"Fran? No. Neither did Paul. But somebody was here in the early afternoon, around one o'clock."

"How do you know that?"

"Mrs. Cappicotti, my neighbor across the street. One of the few people in this neighborhood who don't think I'm some kind of monster. She went out to walk the family dog just as a car was pulling into the garage."

"What kind of car?"

"A light-colored car. She thought it must be mine. She only got a glimpse of it — the garage door came down as soon as the car was inside."

I ruminated on that. "So whoever it was had to have a remote door opener."

"I guess so. There are only two, one in my car, the spare in a kitchen drawer. But that one's gone now; I can't find it anywhere. Whoever took Alice must've found it — it's the only way the door could've been opened or closed from outside."

"Is the garage on the security system?"

"No. Only the inside door to the kitchen is wired."

"Is there an outside door?"

"Yes, but it has a bolt lock. I checked it — it hadn't been tampered with."

Lock picking isn't the only way to get through a locked door. A skeleton key will do the job, depending on the type of lock.

"One o'clock, you said. Can you account for your whereabouts at that time?"

"Not to anybody's satisfaction," Cahill said. "I took a late lunch that day, by myself. Bought an In-N-Out burger, drove over to Community Park to eat it. I was feeling a little stressed, Alice and the demands of my job, and I just wanted to be alone for a while."

He brooded into his glass again, his fingers clenching and unclenching around it. I could see that he wanted a refill and was struggling against the need. I expected him to lose the struggle, say something, and pop to his feet again, but he didn't. He set the tumbler down on the table, pushed it away with his fingertips, and then looked at me again.

"You see the kind of bind I'm in, why I'm so confused and upset? It all sounds unbelievable, I know that, but everything I've told you is the truth; I swear it."

I didn't say anything.

"I need somebody to believe in me," he said, "and not just to get myself off the hook with the police. I need to know what happened to Alice, have her found and brought back home if she hasn't been . . . if she's all right. That's the most important thing." He drew a tremulous breath. "*Do* you believe me?"

Good question. The desperate appeal in his voice sounded genuine; he had looked and acted sincere throughout the interview, seemed to honestly care about his wife's well-being over and above his own. But I had been fooled on more than one occasion by accomplished liars looking to use me for their own ends — the guy in Atherton, most recently, and the story he'd told had been a hell of a lot less credible than Cahill's. I'd made the mistake of buying into that one, if not for long, and lived to regret it, and it had made me even more leery and cynical.

On the other hand, if Cahill was responsible for his wife's disappearance, what did he have to gain, really, by retaining a private detective? It wouldn't take much, if any, of the heat off him. Could work against him, in fact, to have another trained professional snooping around. The only way I could see that his motive made sense was if his story was more or less straight, if he really was innocent.

"Will you help me?" He extended a hand, palm up, almost as if in supplication. "Please?"

By way of answer I took out the standard agency contract I'd brought with me. He read it over quickly, gave me a grateful look, and signed and returned it.

I got to my feet. "Suppose you show me around, Mr. Cahill. Starting with the outside garage door."

2

The lock on the garage door was a stainless-steel dead bolt of good-quality Japanese manufacture. The only key to it, Cahill said, was the one he kept on his key ring. I examined the keyhole, bolt, plate. No tampering marks, as he'd indicated. But that didn't mean the lock was immune to a skeleton key.

The door into the kitchen was the heavy-duty variety; its lock bore no telltale scratches, either. We went back inside and I had a look at the locks on the other doors. Double dead bolts on both the front and back, the doors themselves also heavy-duty and tightly fitted into their frames. Likewise the windows in the kitchen, family room, living room, utility room. With the alarm system armed, the house was about as secure as you can make a private residence these days.

We saved Alice Cahill's office until last. It

was at a rear corner of the ground floor, behind the family room. One of those large enclosures designed for no particular purpose — office, den, recreation room, spare bedroom, kids' playroom, whatever the owner cared to make of it. It was shrouded in gloom, which Cahill chased by flicking a wall switch as we entered. There were windows in the back wall and one side wall, both tightly covered with thick venetian blinds so that little daylight could penetrate.

"Alice always keeps the windows covered like that," Cahill said. He seemed less edgy now that I'd agreed to take his case, but the facial muscle still ticced. "She doesn't even like to look outdoors into the garden."

The furnishings were all dark wood. A computer workstation sat in the middle of a thick-pile carpet, positioned at an angle so that when Mrs. Cahill occupied the brown leather desk chair her back would be to the blinded windows; the workstation held a printer and a desk lamp but no computer. Next to it stood a desk with not much on it except a thick, padded shipping envelope, a couple of plastic paper trays; next to the desk was a leather recliner, a floor lamp, and a boom-box portable radio on a spindly table. Most of the inner wall was spanned by a bookcase, its shelves filled with paperback books and a plastic case of the sort that holds CDs and DVDs.

"I don't see a computer," I said. "Does your wife do all of her writing on the missing laptop?"

"Yes. She has an iPad, too. The police confiscated it and my iPad. Fat lot of good it did them." He added with some bitterness, "They haven't returned them yet."

He went to the desk, presumably for the e-mail printouts he'd told me about. But the padded bag caught his eye and he paused to pick it up. "This came the day she vanished — it was on the front porch when I got home. Copies of her latest novel, I think. I haven't had the heart to open it." He shook his head, set the bag down again, and opened the bottom drawer of the desk. While he was doing that, I pulled the blinds back on each of the windows to check the locks. As secure as the rest.

Cahill handed me a manila folder labeled **Dellbrook**. There were three e-mails signed by Grace Dellbrook, the first dated a little more than two weeks ago, the most recent two days before Alice Cahill was last seen; if another one had been received the morning of her disappearance, she had not printed it out. There were only two replies from Mrs. Cahill. I read them over in order received and answered. Dellbrook's initial communication was fairly long, angry but controlled and nonthreatening, claiming that Alice Cahill's novel *The Convenient Bride* was a plagiarism of her, Dellbrook's, two-year-old novel, *What the Bride Found Out.* Several points of similarity were cited as proof — San Francisco setting, plot and character development, the climactic scene.

Mrs. Cahill emphatically denied the charge. She had never read or heard of *What the Bride Found Out,* the cited similarities were coincidental and relatively minor, if in fact they existed at all, and she did not appreciate being accused of a crime she hadn't committed. Curt and dismissive, but not provocative.

The other two Dellbrook e-mails showed escalating hostility. In the second she cited other similarities between her book and Mrs. Cahill's, all of which were disputed and refuted as "utter nonsense." The third demanded an admission of guilt, an apology, and "a suitable financial settlement" and threatened "dire consequences" if they weren't forthcoming. Presumably that meant contacting Alice Cahill's publisher and perhaps an attorney.

"You see what I mean by a nutcase?" Cahill said when I finished reading. "People like that crawl out of the woodwork when they think they can scam some money."

"Did you show these to the police?"

"Yes, for all the good it did. The cop in charge, a lieutenant named Kowalski, barely glanced at them. Too focused on me as a suspect."

I got Cahill's permission to borrow the file. Then I asked him, "How do you suppose the woman got your wife's e-mail address?"

"From Alice's website. She made the mistake of including it so her fans could get in touch with her."

"Your home address included, too?"

"No. But it's not too hard to find out where somebody lives these days, is it?"

I agreed that it wasn't. "What was your wife planning to do about the threats?"

"I don't know," he said.

"Didn't she discuss them with you?"

"No. She didn't say anything at all to me about these ridiculous accusations. I wish she had. But she can be . . . well, closed off when something upsets her."

"If she didn't tell you, how did you find out?"

"I came across the e-mail file in her desk a few days ago." The admission was apologetic. "We have a pact: I don't intrude on her privacy and she doesn't intrude on mine. But the way things are . . . I looked through her files hoping to find something that would explain what happened to her. This is all there is that might have any bearing on it."

I said, "In her second reply, she mentions having bought a copy of the Dellbrook novel online. I'd like to see it if it's still here."

"It is. In the bookcase."

I went over there with him. While he hunted for *What the Bride Found Out,* I looked over the other books. Reference books, two shelves of modern and historical romance paperbacks, and one shelf of Alice Cahill's novels under her own name and the Jennifer West pseudonym, multiple copies of each.

"Here it is," Cahill said. He pulled out a somewhat shabby copy of a paperback with a black-and-white cover illustration that might have been drawn by a semi-talented third-grader.

I opened it and looked at the first sentence — "Doreen was as thrilled as a new bride must always be on her wedding day, her heart beating fast, as her thoughts dwelled on the church ceremony and all the wonderfulness that would follow." — and closed it again.

"Piece of crap," Cahill said. "Alice's writing is ten times better."

"You read all of her books?"

"Well . . . no. I read the first couple, as a favor to her, but that kind of stuff . . ." He shrugged and finished lamely, "I'm not much of a reader."

"All right with you if I borrow this, too? And a copy of *The Convenient Bride*?"

"Sure. Help yourself. You're going to talk to the Dellbrook woman, right? If you can find her?"

"I can find her." I transferred a copy of *The Convenient Bride* from the shelf to my coat pocket, tucked *What the Bride Found Out* in there with it. Then I said, "I have to ask this question. Did your wife have any other enemies you know of?"

"No. How could she, cooped up in here the way she was?"

"No problems with her sister, the doctor, her college friend?"

"Not the way you mean. Some friction, sure — like I said before, it's not easy dealing with a panicky agoraphobe. She and Kendra were always sniping at each other — Kendra's the bossy, preachy type — but they've been doing that ever since they were kids." He sighed heavily. "Besides, it couldn't have been any of them driving that

31

car Mrs. Cappicotti saw. I'm the only one who can't prove where I was around one o'clock that day."

I let it drop for now. "Tell me some more about the accident she was involved in. You said the passenger in the other vehicle was killed, the driver injured. How badly injured?"

"Broken leg, concussion."

"Man or woman?"

"A Pleasant Hill woman named Hernandez, Sofia Hernandez. Her father was the one killed. But if you're thinking she bore a grudge, she didn't. No civil suit for negligence or anything like that. We paid all her hospital bills and the funeral expenses."

"Did you or your wife have any direct contact with her?"

"No. It was all done through the insurance people and our attorney."

"No communication from her since?"

"Not that I know about. Alice would have told me if she'd heard from her." Cahill wagged his head again. "More than four years. You can't be thinking the Hernandez woman is responsible for Alice's disappearance after all that time?"

"It's not likely, no, but stranger things have happened. I'm just trying to cover all the bases."

I wrote "Sofia Hernandez, last known living Pleasant Hill 4 yrs ago" in my notebook. Also the contact information for Kendra and Paul Nesbitt and Fran Woodward, which Cahill supplied, and the full name of the police lieutenant in charge of the official investigation, Frank Kowalski. When I was done, I asked Cahill for a recent photograph of his wife. He said he had a good one in his office upstairs.

His office, a converted bedroom, wasn't half as neat or well appointed as hers. Mismatched furniture, his computer on a stand next to a small limed-oak desk. The photo of his wife he gave me was the one on the desk, a head and shoulders color portrait. "Don't worry," he said as he removed it from the frame. "I have another one just like it."

"How recent is it?"

"Five years, but she hasn't changed that much . . . physically."

Alice Cahill was a slender, olive-skinned brunette, pretty in a snub-nosed, gamin sort of way. Her eyes were her best feature, slightly slanted so that they gave her face a faintly Asian look, the pupils so dark they seemed almost black. In the photo the eyes had a mischievous gleam. It would be gone now if she was still alive, I thought. Four years gone.

In addition to the converted office, there were a master suite and another bedroom upstairs. The door to the second bedroom was open and I could see an unmade bed and a scattering of his clothing inside. "Alice and I have separate rooms," he said as we passed it. "She sleeps in the master bedroom." I nodded and made no comment, but he seemed to need to explain further, the tic along his jaw jumping and fluttering. "Before the accident we had an active sex life. Afterward . . . only now and then, and on her initiative. The past six months, not at all . . ."

I said, "That's none of my business, Mr. Cahill, unless it has some relevance."

"It doesn't, but Alice blabbed about it to Kendra and Kendra told the cops. Supposedly another motive for me wanting to do away with her. I . . . thought you should know."

Everything in the master bedroom was in perfect order. Compulsive housekeeping, I thought. I saw no need to poke around in the various drawers and the big walk-in closet — Cahill and the police would have done that, and he'd have told me if anything relevant had been found — but I did take a quick look into the closet. There were relatively few items of clothing, most of them casual wear; the reason, Cahill said, was that his wife had insisted on downsizing her wardrobe after the accident. She had given away most of her jewelry, too, to charity outlets. Another indication of the depth of her guilt over the death she'd inadvertently caused.

I'd spent enough time here, gathered more than enough information to begin my investigation. Cahill and I went downstairs. He stepped out onto the porch with me. I told him I'd be in touch as soon as I had anything to report, and we were shaking hands when he glanced past me and said, "Oh, there's Mrs. Cappicotti, the neighbor I told you about."

I turned to see a woman coming down the front walk of the house opposite, a smallish brown-and-white dog on a leash pulling her along. "You want to talk to her now?" Cahill asked. "I'll go over with you —"

I did want to talk to her, but alone. "No need for that, as long as she's approachable."

"She is. Nice old lady, a little feisty sometimes."

The woman had stopped on the sidewalk to look over at Cahill and me. I said goodbye to him and went down and across the street. The woman was around my age, maybe a little older, with wispy gray hair poking out from under a knit cap. She had a lean, rosy-cheeked face, wore a pair of blue-rimmed glasses with thick lenses. The day was warmish, but she was bundled up in a coat and paisley scarf. Wrapped around her left hand was a plastic Baggie, all set to do her part to keep the streets of Shelter Hills Estates clean.

The dog was jumping around, panting noisily. I kept a wary eye on him as I came up — I've had run-ins with dogs before — but this one seemed tame enough and showed no interest in me.

"Mrs. Cappicotti?"

"That's me. Don't worry about him, he doesn't bite. You another policeman?"

"No, ma'am. Private investigator." I showed her the photostat of my license.

"Working for Mr. Cahill, eh? Well, he must've got himself a good one if you're still in business, man your age. That why you're not retired?"

There wasn't any point in telling her I was semiretired. "I'd rather work than sit around on my fanny all day."

She liked that; she made a chuckling sound, exposing dentures so white they must have been fairly new. "Exactly how I feel," she said. "I was in the insurance business, but the damn company had a mandatory retirement age. Now I do volunteer work — hospice, Senior Center, county food bank — and run the household for my daughter and her family. That's why I'm living here with them instead of —" The brown-and-white dog kept yanking at the leash, eager to get on with the walk. "All right, Spots, all right," she said to the pooch. Then to me, "Spots. Stupid name for a dog. But my granddaughter named him, so what can you do?"

"Nice-looking animal. What breed is he?"

"Jack Russell terrier. Gentle enough, but he's a pain in the ass sometimes. I prefer cats. Got two of those in the house, too."

I said, "I'd like to ask you a few questions, Mrs. Cappicotti, if you wouldn't mind."

"About that car I saw over at the Cahills', I suppose."

"Yes."

"Okay, but you'll have to ask 'em while I walk this beast. He's about to yank my arm out of the socket."

I nodded, fell into step with her as she set off. "Mr. Cahill told me you saw the car drive into his garage about one o'clock the day his wife disappeared."

"Not exactly. It was already inside when I came out with Spots here. I just got a glimpse of its hind end before the door came down."

"And it was light colored?"

"White or beige or light tan. My eyesight isn't what it used to be, and I just had a glimpse, like I said." She added, her upper lip curling disdainfully, "The policeman I talked to seemed to think I might not have seen a car at all, that it was just my imagination. Idiot. I don't have that kind of imagination and I'm a long way from being senile."

"Could it have been Mr. Cahill's BMW?"

"Could've been, but he says it wasn't and I believe him. Whatever happened to his wife, I don't think he had anything to do with it. I'm in the minority there, even my daughter and her husband think he did, but I know people and he's not capable of it. Good neighbor, friendly. Never complained about having to carry that heavy cross of his — his wife not being able to leave the house, I mean."

"So as far as you know, the two of them got along."

"As well as could be expected, the situation being what it was. Heard her screaming at him a couple of times, I guess when she had one of her panic attacks, but never once heard him raise his voice to her."

Spots stopped sniffing around bushes and posts and pillars, investigated a small curb-side tree, decided it was suitable, and proceeded to pee on it. "So much for number one," Mrs. Cappicotti said approvingly. "Now if he'll just get on with number two."

"The day of the disappearance," I said. "Did you see any other vehicles in the Cahills' driveway or parked in front of the house?"

"The sister's car was there when I went out to do some weeding in the garden around half past ten. I know it because she came around fairly often."

"How long did she stay, do you know?"

"Half hour or so. I was still weeding when she left."

"What color and make is her car?"

"White. I don't know from makes or models. Four doors and new looking, that's all I can tell you."

"Do you know her at all?"

"To talk to? No. Tried once, but she snooted me. The kind of woman men like — pretty face, big boobs — but about as friendly as a shark."

"Mrs. Cahill had other visitors from time

to time," I said. "Her brother-in-law, a friend of hers named Fran Woodward. Do you remember the colors of their vehicles?"

"Not off hand . . . No, wait, the doctor's is white, too, I think."

"Have you had conversations with either of them?"

"Him a couple of times, he seems all right. Never had any reason to talk to the friend. Kind of weird, that one."

"How do you mean, weird?"

"Different color hair every time I see her, and I don't mean black, brown, or yellow. Chartreuse, turquoise, henna red. Dresses like some sort of New Age hippie."

"Did anyone else come to visit Alice Cahill? During the day, I mean, while her husband was away?"

"Not that I ever saw when I was home — Well, finally!"

We were in the middle of the next block by this time, and Spots had stopped again and was squatting on a patch of curbside lawn. But then he stood up and trotted off again without leaving anything on the grass.

"Damn dog. Come on, you," she snapped at him, "get it over with." He paid no attention to her. "I swear he does this on purpose just to annoy me. Once he dragged me around for six blocks before he did his business. I'm spry for my age, but not that spry. There ought to be a command."

"Command?"

"You know, a training command. They've got one for everything else and he obeys them. I say shake hands, he shakes hands. I say roll over, he rolls over. I say sit up, he sits up. I say poop, he either looks at me like I've got three heads or ignores me completely. If somebody invented a go poop command it'd sure make dog walking a lot easier."

"Sounds like a good idea to me," I said.

Spots evidently thought so, too. As soon as Mrs. Cappicotti said the words, "Go poop," he squatted and did exactly that.

3

JAKE RUNYON

Runyon liked to drive. Always had, in recent years to the point of compulsion, if not obsession. When Colleen was alive, they'd taken all sorts of long and short driving trips together. During his time on the Seattle PD he'd done most of the driving while in uniform and again after he was promoted. He should have been behind the wheel instead of his detective partner, Ron Cain, in the high-speed chase after a fugitive homicide suspect; if he had been, maybe, just maybe, he could have avoided the truck that came out of nowhere and slammed into them, killing Ron and putting him in the hospital with the triple-fractured tibia that had required two surgeries, given him a permanent if barely noticeable limp, and ended his police career.

After the goddamn ovarian cancer ripped Colleen away from him and he'd gone to work as an investigator for Caldwell & Associates, he'd been on the road a lot as part of the job and also started taking long weekend and nighttime drives. That pattern had escalated after he'd moved down to San Francisco in the abortive effort to reconnect with his estranged son, Joshua, and gotten the field operative's job with Bill and Tamara's firm. He'd traveled every major road in the Greater Bay Area and beyond the past five years, using up downtime and logging thousands of miles familiarizing himself with his new home turf.

During those six terrible months while Colleen slowly wasted away, driving helped him develop the ability to shut himself down without losing awareness — a kind of catlike patience that kept external forces beyond his control from touching him, kept the pain and memories more or less at bay. Didn't matter where he went or why. Being on the move satisfied his restless need for activity, gave him a measure of peace that he hardly ever found when caught between four walls. When he stepped out of the Ford after a long drive, he was calm, focused, ready to face another day and whatever tasks went with it.

So he was always glad when assigned to a case that required a road trip, as this one to

Eagle Lake in the Sierras did. He'd never been there before, had never even heard of the place, but that didn't matter. Rural, urban, suburban — all the same to him. After Colleen's death, he'd lost all interest in his surroundings except as they pertained to his work and to bare-bones living; towns, roads, routes, neighborhoods, landmarks had all been visually noted and then filed away in a corner of his mind for future business-related reference. Eagle Lake would be no different.

He preferred his road trips to be solitary, but the fact that he had a passenger on the first leg of this one was all right with him. It might have bothered him a little if the woman, Patricia Dennison, had been the chatty type, but she wasn't. She hadn't said more than twenty words since he'd picked her up at her Marina District home at eight that morning, and they were now a little less than halfway to their destination. She'd maintained the same position the entire time, over close to the passenger door with her hands folded in her lap, her eyes straight ahead but her attention focused inward. Typical of a recent widow, the more so given the circumstances of her husband's death and the mission she and Runyon were on.

The investigative part of it shaped up to

be fairly routine, not that that mattered to Runyon. A case was a case, some stimulating, some dull, all part of the job. Philip Dennison had been found dead inside a cabin on Eagle Lake, a mile or so from the village of the same name. His death was accidental; there didn't seem to be any doubt of that, considering that he'd been alone in the cabin with all the doors and windows locked on the inside. The question was what he'd been doing there in the first place. When he'd left San Francisco the previous Friday, he'd told his wife he was headed for a sales conference — he'd been a sales rep for a computer software firm — in Southern California, several hundred miles in the opposite direction.

The officer in charge of the sheriff's substation in Eagle Lake, a senior deputy named Rittenhouse, hadn't been able to provide an answer. Nothing in the cabin or in Dennison's vehicle explained it; the only luggage was his, he'd brought no sporting gear with him, and there were no indications that he'd had company during the time he'd been there. None of the locals were able to shed light on the matter. Nor had any of the dead man's friends and coworkers Mrs. Dennison had spoken to. As far as she or they knew, he hadn't known anybody in the Eagle Lake area. And she, like Runyon, had never been to or heard of the place before.

Naturally she wanted the matter looked into. Closure. That was one reason, the primary one, she'd come to the agency. The other reasons were to see this unknown place where her husband had died, to make arrangements for the transportation of his remains to the Bay Area for burial, and to take possession of his Cadillac and drive it back to the city for disposal. Unless there were complications, Runyon figured he'd be making his solo return trip by Saturday at the latest.

They were on Highway 50 just outside Sacramento when Mrs. Dennison stirred and then abruptly broke her silence. As if giving voice to a brooding thought, she said, "I think he was with a woman up there."

Runyon glanced over at her. "Your husband?"

"Yes. It has to be the reason Philip went to Eagle Lake. To fuck some woman."

Runyon was used to hearing casual obscenities from women as well as men, but this one wasn't casual. It came out low and brittle, as though the taste of it in her mouth was unfamiliar, sour. Not a word she used very often, he thought, and a measure of the depth of her feelings.

"From what you told us yesterday, the Eagle Lake authorities seemed to think he was alone."

"They said there were no traces of a woman in the cabin where he died, but that doesn't mean there wasn't one. I don't believe he was alone."

"What makes you so sure?"

"Why else would he go up there, hundreds of miles from where he told me he was going." It wasn't a question.

"Maybe he just wanted to get away by himself for a few days."

"He wanted to get away, yes, but not by himself. Not Philip."

"He's done something similar before, is that what you're saying?"

"Twice. At least twice."

"You know this for a fact?"

"I know it," she said. "He was discreet about it, oh, very discreet. He never cheated in his own backyard; he always had to sneak away to do it."

"Different women, do you think, or the same one?"

"I don't know. Different ones, I suppose." Her mouth quirked. "He always used to say variety is the spice of life. He was talking about other things, but the implication is the same."

"Did you accuse him of being unfaithful?"

"Yes. He denied it, of course, but he wasn't a convincing liar. I told him I'd divorce him if I ever had sufficient proof. It scared him — he loved me; he didn't want to lose me — but he kept on doing it just the same."

Serial philanderer. Some men were wired that way, even those with wives as attractive as Patricia Dennison. She'd given her age as thirty-two, but she could have passed for seven or eight years younger. Flawless skin with no visible age lines, dark blond hair framing a heart-shaped face, cornflower-blue eyes. Impersonal appraisal: Runyon had never allowed himself to consider a client as anything but a client and never would.

He said, "You must have loved him to put up with it."

"Once." Then, after a long pause, "No, that's not true. I still loved him, just not as much."

"Would you have gone through with a divorce?"

"Oh, yes. It wasn't an idle threat."

Runyon was silent.

Pretty soon Mrs. Dennison said, "I want you to find out who he was with at the lake. Her name, where she lives."

"For what reason?"

"I have some things to say to her."

"You realize that if there was a woman —"

"There was."

"— she may not have known he was married."

"That doesn't matter."

"Confronting her would serve no real purpose, Mrs. Dennison."

"Please don't try to talk me out of it. Will you find her for me or not?"

Not a commitment he could make yet; it wasn't part of her original statement of purpose in hiring him through the agency. He let a few seconds tick away before he said carefully, "If it's possible, I'd want to be there when you talk to her."

She smiled — a brief, counterfeit smile. "Why? Do you suppose I mean to scratch her eyes out or shoot her or something?"

"I don't suppose anything," Runyon said. "It's a matter of protocol."

"All right. If you need to be there, then be there; I don't care. Just find her, that's all I ask."

Eagle Lake was in the El Dorado National Forest a few miles northeast of Highway 50, some two-thirds of the way to South

Lake Tahoe. The village was wrapped part-way around the southern tip of the lake, a glass-smooth body of water a mile or so in diameter. From the glimpses Runyon had of it coming in, the lake was tightly hemmed by pines all the way around; short docks and portions of summer homes and permanent residences were visible here and there. A line of steep hills and high mountain peaks rose beyond the far end of the village, ski runs carved out of two of the closest hillsides. The village buildings seemed to be mostly A-frames, the major exceptions a couple of lodges near the ski areas, the largest designed to imitate a Swiss chalet.

All in all, it was one of those off-the-beaten-track mountain communities that offered water sports in the summer and snow sports in the winter. If it had a chamber of commerce, the word they'd use to describe it would probably be *picturesque.* To Runyon it was just another place to catalogue and eventually tuck away with the multitude of others in his mental filing cabinet.

It was a few minutes past noon when he drove past a sign on the outskirts that gave the population as 1,026. There was plenty of snow on the peaks near and far, and leftover patches of it spotted the hillsides and shaded hollows alongside the two-lane road and Eagle Lake's main street that intersected it. The village had a semi-deserted look and feel. Between seasons, the winter people gone and the summer people yet to arrive.

A café appeared ahead and Runyon asked Patricia Dennison if she wanted to stop for something to eat before they spoke with Deputy Rittenhouse. She said no, she wasn't hungry, she just wanted to get that part of it over with as quickly as possible.

The sheriff's station was easy enough to find, a large log A-frame set back from the road with a tall sign at the entrance to an asphalt parking lot in front. Runyon pulled the Ford in next to a pair of blue-and-white cruisers marked **Eagle Lake Sheriff Department**.

The day was mostly sunny, but the wind that stung his face when he stepped out still held a winter chill. Mrs. Dennison seemed not to notice. She left her coat unbuttoned, her wide mouth set in a grimly determined line, as they entered the building.

Typical small-town substation: three desks with computers, communication equipment, locked case of rifles and shotguns on one wall, closed door to what was probably a private office at the rear, railed divider separating the working part of the office from the visitors' section. One rack of antlers on a large wall-mounted moose head was doing service as a coat and scarf rack.

Only one of the desks had an occupant, a fortyish woman dressed in a khaki uniform. Civilian dispatcher, probably. She smiled at them. "Hello, folks. Can I help you?"

"I'm Patricia Dennison. Deputy Rittenhouse is expecting me."

The woman's expression turned solemn. "Oh, yes. He had to go out, but he shouldn't be far away. I'll radio him you're here."

She did that, spoke briefly, and then informed them that the chief deputy would be there in about ten minutes. Patricia Dennison refused an offer of coffee while they waited; Runyon did likewise. They sat in silence on a bench in the visitors' area.

Nine minutes by the wall clock had ticked by when Deputy Rittenhouse came in. He was a heavyset man in his fifties, his large egg-shaped head barren except for a few tufts of light brown hair and a small inflamed patch above his forehead that was probably eczema. He wore a badge pinned to his uniform shirt, a radio communicator hooked over the collar, a Sam Browne belt around his thick waist.

The introductions out of the way, Rittenhouse invited them into his office where they could speak in private. He spoke softly, gravely, in deference to the widow, but Runyon had the impression that he could be a no-nonsense type when the situation called for it. Mrs. Dennison had told him when she made the appointment that she was bringing a private investigator with her, but not the reason why. Rittenhouse's appraisal of Runyon was brief and sharp-eyed. Small-town law officers weren't always happy to have PIs on their turf, but if the deputy had any such feelings, he didn't allow them to show.

"I imagine you'll want to get the most unpleasant business out of the way first," he said to Mrs. Dennison. "Official identification, transportation arrangements. Your husband's remains are at Eagle Lake Clinic, not far from here —"

"No," she said. "That can wait."

"Wait? I don't understand."

"I'd like to see the cabin where he died first."

". . . For what purpose?"

"There's no reason I can't see it, is there?"

"No, but . . ." Rittenhouse rubbed at the inflamed patch on his scalp with a blunt forefinger. "As I told you when we spoke on the phone, there's no question that his death was accidental. All the doors and windows were locked and barred on the inside."

"That's not why I want to see the cabin."

"Well, as I told you on the phone, no one had been there with him. At any time before the accident, I mean."

"Then why did he come all the way up here when he was supposed to be at a conference in Los Angeles for five days?"

"I have no idea." Maybe not, but Rittenhouse's manner had changed slightly, as if the subject made him uneasy. "Is that why you hired Mr. Runyon here? To find out why your husband came to Eagle Lake?"

"That's my business."

"Well, he could have had any number of reasons." Innocent reasons, Rittenhouse's tone implied. When she didn't respond, he said lamely, "Sometimes people do things that don't make sense to anybody but them."

Runyon said, "Mind if I ask a question, Deputy?"

"Go ahead."

"Who did Mr. Dennison rent the cabin from?"

"He didn't rent it. The owner gave him permission to stay there."

"Who would the owner be?"

"Man named Hansen, Lloyd Hansen.

Insurance agent, lives down in Sacramento."

"Have you talked to him?"

"Yes. He confirmed it. Mr. Dennison stopped to get the key on his way up Friday afternoon."

"How do the two of them know each other?"

"Old friends from college."

Runyon asked the client if Lloyd Hansen's name was familiar. She said in a flat voice, "Yes, Philip mentioned him. Now and then they would get together for what he called a reunion."

"Did you ever meet him?"

"No. As far as I know he never came to San Francisco."

Runyon asked the deputy, "Did Hansen have any idea why Mr. Dennison wanted use of the cabin?"

"No."

"Had Mr. Dennison ever asked to use it before?"

"He didn't say. And I saw no reason to ask him."

Patricia Dennison shifted impatiently on her chair. "May I see the cabin or not?"

"If you insist," Rittenhouse said. "Just to look at it from the outside?"

"No. The inside, too."

"Then I'll have to go with you."

"Can't you just give us the key and tell us how to get there?"

"No, ma'am. I'm afraid that's not possible."

"All right, then. Can we go now?"

Rittenhouse got ponderously to his feet. "I'll get the key," he said, but he didn't look happy about it.

4

On my way out of Shelter Hills I called
Tamara to tell her I was going ahead with
the investigation and give her the details of
my interview with James Cahill. It's against
the law in California to talk on a cell phone
while you're operating a motor vehicle, as it
damn well should be, unless you use one of
those hands-free Bluetooth devices. Tamara
and Kerry had talked me into getting one,
and I had to admit it made the job of com-
municating when on the road easier. But I
still felt self-conscious wearing headphones
and speaking into a mouthpiece while alone
in the car. I could just imagine somebody in
a passing car looking over at me and thinking I was one of those strange types who
would benefit from psychiatric treatment.

"I already know what I'm going to label
the file," she said. " 'The Case of the Absent
Agoraphobe.' Like one of those old Perry
Mason TV shows."

"Since when do you watch old Perry Mason episodes?"

"Long time now. Whenever I wake up in the middle of the night and can't get back to sleep. Seems like there's always one on some channel or another. Hey, I'm getting to like black-and-white."

"Too bad more people your age don't feel the same."

"Goes for other things, too," she said pointedly. "You want me to run a check on the new client and his wife both?"

"Yes. I'm fairly sure Cahill was straight with me, but I'm not taking anything for granted anymore. See what you can find on the accident four years ago, and the present whereabouts of the daughter of the man who was killed, Sofia Hernandez, last known address Pleasant Hill. And the address of the woman who accused Alice Cahill of plagiarism, Grace Dellbrook."

"Dellbrook spelled how?"

"Just like it sounds. D-e-l-l-b-r-o-o-k."

"Got it."

"Kendra Nesbitt, Dr. Paul Nesbitt, and Fran Woodward, too. The field of known suspects seems pretty narrow, so we'll need to cover them all."

"*Known* being the operative word. Doesn't have to be one of them who made the woman disappear."

"No, it doesn't. But if it's not, and no other prospects turn up, James Cahill may well wind up on the wrong end of a murder charge."

"You think Mrs. Cahill is dead, then?"

"I hope not. But it's been a week. She wasn't kidnapped for ransom or there'd have been communication by this time. It's barely possible she was snatched by a psycho bent on torture and is being held captive somewhere, but I don't buy it." Didn't want to buy it, after the monstrous thing that had happened to Kerry in Green Valley not so long ago.

"There are other kinds of psychos than the sex kind," Tamara said. "The Dellbrook woman could be one of them."

"Yes, she could," I said. "Start the checks with her. Meanwhile I'll see what I can find out from Alice Cahill's sister."

The Nesbitts lived in Lafayette, Walnut Creek's affluent neighbor to the west. The GPS I'd had installed in the car a while back got me to their address without any difficulty. One more piece of modern technology I'd resisted until it became a necessity, like iPhones and the Bluetooth, and that I had to admit made life a little easier

— when they worked as they were supposed to. Adapt or stagnate, that had been Kerry's advice. Well, she was right, of course. But I couldn't help being nostalgic for the old ways I'd learned and understood and functioned pretty well with and by, and I still clung stubbornly to the ones that had yet to disappear or be subsumed.

The neighborhood, as you'd expect an established physician and his wife to reside in, was a very good one. Large homes on large lots, some with lawns that were still green in spite of the drought restrictions on water usage. Well-to-do scofflaws are much worse than poor ones, in my opinion. Their "I can afford to pay for it, so why should I bother to conserve" attitude irritates the hell out of me. Call it contempt for the contemptuous.

Dr. and Mrs. Nesbitt were not among the offenders, at least not where the maintenance of green lawns was concerned. Their landscaping was a fairly low-maintenance array of trees large and small, rhododendrons, rosebushes, and other flowering shrubs and plants. Not that that absolved them from being water wasters; all the plantings had the kind of healthy look homeowners get when they keep their sprinkler system turned on six or seven days a week. The yard was being tended to by two people when the disembodied GPS voice told me I'd arrived at my destination — a middle-aged Hispanic who was probably the owner of the vehicle labeled **Pedro's Gardening Service** parked in front, and a younger woman wearing old clothes and a straw hat.

A cream-colored four-door Lexus, new or almost new, was parked in the driveway. I walked up past it, turned into the yard on a flagstone path. The woman had been industriously using a pair of clippers on one of the rosebushes; she stopped when she saw me, stood peering for a few seconds, then came over to greet me.

She had the kind of big-boned figure that had probably once been voluptuous — the loose gardening shirt she wore didn't hide the fact that she was well endowed above the waist — but was now a little on the heavy side. The broad, floppy brim of the hat shadowed her face, but I could see enough of it to tell that she was in her mid- to late thirties and that the extra weight did not detract from her appeal. Even dressed in gardening clothes, she wore a dark red shade of lipstick.

"Yes?"

"Mrs. Nesbitt? Kendra Nesbitt?"

"That's right. Who are you?"

I told her and then showed her. Her expression had been neutral until she had a good look at the license photostat; then it tightened, her rouged lips compressing.

"A private detective," she said. Her tone had changed, too, developed a coating of frost. "I suppose he hired you. My brother-in-law."

"James Cahill, yes."

"To find out what happened to my sister."

"That's right."

"Well, it won't do him any good. Won't convince anyone he's not responsible for Alice going missing, least of all the police."

"*Responsible* meaning what, exactly?"

"What do you think it means? He killed her."

"Why would he do that, Mrs. Nesbitt?"

Her mouth developed a sour pucker that pulled the rest of her face out of shape, turned attractive into unattractive. "Because he hated her, that's why. For being ill, confined to the house. For turning his life upside down and making it what he called a living hell."

"If he felt that way, then why not just divorce her?"

"Because of the insurance, that's why."

"Insurance?"

"Their joint life insurance policy with Statewide Mutual. One hundred thousand dollars. If he divorced her, she'd have changed her beneficiary. Now, he stands to collect."

"Are you suggesting the insurance could be a motive for doing away with her?"

"It's possible, isn't it?"

"But not likely if she remains missing. He'd have to wait seven years until she's declared legally dead in order to collect."

"Seven years isn't all that long a time," Mrs. Nesbitt said. "And if her body should turn up and he's finally arrested, he might be willing to take the chance that some smart lawyer would get him acquitted. Then he'd collect right away. He —"

The rest of what she was about to say was lost in the sudden whining thunder of a leaf blower. Mrs. Nesbitt's mouth shaped the word *Shit;* she stormed away to where Pedro was beginning to swirl leaves and twigs from under one of the taller trees. When she got his attention, she gestured angrily and he shut the thing off in a hurry. I heard her yell at him to keep the damn thing off before she came stomping back to where I was.

"I hate those things," she said. "You can't hear yourself think."

"That makes two of us."

She took off the straw hat, ran the back of her hand across her forehead. She had the same type of olive skin as her sister, her eyes brown and close-set, her brunette hair cut in a short, feathery style; you could see the resemblance, but for my taste, Alice Cahill was the better looking of the two.

"James didn't tell you about the insurance, did he?" Mrs. Nesbitt said. "Made himself out to be a devoted, loving husband. Well, he wasn't. He treated my sister like dirt, especially when he'd been drinking."

"Is he a heavy drinker?"

"Sometimes. And he can be violent when he's drunk."

"You're saying she was afraid of him, then?"

"Of course she was. I tried and tried to convince her she should get him out of the house and out of her life, but she couldn't bring herself to do it. Even though they fought constantly and he threatened to 'put her out of her misery.' Too timid, too afraid of being alone."

"You heard him make that kind of threat?"

"No, Alice told me. And that he tried to strangle her once. He didn't tell you about that, either, did he?"

"Yes, he did. He said the incident happened during one of her anxiety attacks, that he was only trying to embrace her and she misunderstood his intention."

"What a damned liar he is. Did he try to blame someone else for Alice being missing?"

"No, he didn't."

"Clever. He thinks he's being clever." Kendra Nesbitt's mouth twisted again, this time into a sardonic half grin. "I'll bet there's something else he didn't tell you. About him and Megan Sprague."

"Who is Megan Sprague?"

"I thought not. She works with him at Streeter Manufacturing. Of course he didn't want you to know he's been having an affair with her."

"How do you know he was?"

"Never mind how I know. Go ask him if you don't believe me, watch him sweat. Goddamn cheating men."

"Did his wife know?"

"I told her, yes. A couple of weeks ago, when I found out."

"Did she confront him?"

"No. I wanted her to, but she refused. She didn't want to believe it was true."

"You told the police all this?"

"Well, of course. But they said they have to have physical evidence that she's dead and her death was a homicide. He was clever about that, too — whatever he did to her, whatever he did with her body."

"And what do you think that is?"

"How should I know? I just hope somebody finds it soon; that's the only way he'll get what's coming to him." She put the hat back on, adjusted it. "I'll get on with my gardening now."

Indirect order for me to leave. But I was not quite ready yet to terminate the interview. I asked her the same question I'd asked Cahill: What was her sister's state of mind the morning of her disappearance?

"She was upset, panicky. Another argument with James about his affair and he'd threatened her again."

"How long did you stay with her?"

"Not long. A few minutes. She wanted to be alone."

"Did you have any other communication with her that day?"

"No."

"Was she expecting anyone else to come by?"

"No. Too busy finishing another of her silly romance books."

"You don't approve of her writing?"

"The writing, yes, it gave her something to do with her time. But not what she wrote. Trash. She had some talent, she ought to

66

have put it to better use."

"Did you tell her how you felt?"

"Yes, but she wouldn't listen."

"Did she tell you about the plagiarism claim against her?"

"No. Why should she? It's utter nonsense."

"But you do know about it."

"James called me when he found the e-mails. Smoke screen, an attempt to divert suspicion from himself. The police think so, too."

"You and your sister got along well, did you?"

Mrs. Nesbitt bristled. "What kind of question is that?"

"A simple one. No friction between you?"

"Did that bastard tell you there was?"

"He made a reference to sibling rivalry."

"Another of his smoke-screen lies. Alice and I weren't as close as we were before her accident, but we got along fine. Just fine." She made an impatient thrusting motion with the clippers. Then, abruptly, "Are you going to keep working for him, after all I've told you?"

"Yes, ma'am. Until and unless there's a compelling reason not to."

"I just gave you several compelling reasons. Or do you think I'm the liar, not him?"

"I don't think that, no," I said. "I have to

keep an open mind."

"Well, I don't. We have nothing more to discuss, so don't come around here bothering me again. You won't be welcome." She put her back to me and went stomping back to her rosebushes.

Complications. He said, she said. The truth might well be somewhere in between, I thought on my way to the car. Dr. Paul Nesbitt would probably side with his wife, but maybe I could get a clearer handle on matters from Fran Woodward. Cahill's relationship with his wife was a key factor and I needed to get it straight.

Then there were the joint life insurance policy and his alleged affair with his co-worker to be considered. One hundred thousand dollars is a lot of money, but it's a pretty thin motive for murder when you have to wait seven years to collect. Very few have that kind of patience when it comes to a large sum of money. And if Cahill had killed his wife, he'd surely have done it in a way that took all suspicion off him — made it look like some kind of accident, one in which the body was found more or less immediately so he could collect the insurance right away.

Involvement with another woman was a motive only if you mixed in other factors.

Cahill might be sleeping with this Megan Sprague, but it didn't have to be anything more than a casual affair; he'd admitted that he and his wife hadn't had relations in the last six months, and sexual deprivation coupled with a difficult home life were impetus for some men to look elsewhere. Even if the relationship was a serious love match, a simple divorce made more sense than violence unless Cahill did in fact hate his wife enough to want her dead. But then we were back to the question I'd asked myself earlier: If he'd killed her, whether with premeditation or in a fit of rage, drunken or otherwise, what could he hope to gain by hiring a private investigator?

It was pretty clear that Cahill hadn't told me about the affair because he was afraid it would give me cause not to take his case. Same with the insurance, maybe. I would continue to work on his behalf, at least until I had another talk with him, but I'd already marked him down a couple of notches for not being completely open with me. Clients who withhold information, whatever their reason, always make me wary and distrustful.

5

JAKE RUNYON

The cabin where Philip Dennison had died was off an unpaved road on the far side of Eagle Lake, a mile or so from the village. A fairly small A-frame built of unpeeled logs, the roof sections steeply pitched, it was situated on a low rise close above the curving shoreline. Pines rimmed it closely on one side; a meadow in which wildflowers grew stretched along the other. The place wasn't isolated; the road passed another, larger A-frame a fifth of a mile distant, and the dock belonging to another, tree-hidden cottage was visible about the same distance farther along.

Deputy Rittenhouse pulled into the lower part of the meadow, stopped in front of an open-front, slant-roofed lean-to that served as a parking shelter. Patricia Dennison had wanted them to take two vehicles, Runyon driving her, but Rittenhouse had insisted that they all go in his cruiser. Nobody had said a word on the short ride from the substation. Runyon had questions, but he didn't want to ask them in front of the client.

When they left the cruiser and started up a slight slope toward the cabin, he had a view of the window in the near-side wall. A short length of new-looking plywood had been nailed across its lower half.

Rittenhouse noticed his glance in that direction. "We had to break the window to get inside," he said. "Front door was barred, back doors and windows all locked tight."

"Barred? Is that usual up here?"

"Not usual, no, but some folks, especially second-homers, are security conscious even when they're in residence." He smiled faintly. "Afraid of bears and Bigfoot, I guess."

Mrs. Dennison was paying no attention to either of them but striding ahead, her gaze fixed on the cabin. There was a porch across the front of it facing the lake, a large window alongside the door with louvered shutters closed on the inside; a nearby path led down to a short dock. She was already standing on the porch when they reached the steps. Her face, set in tight lines, showed nothing of what she was thinking or might be feeling.

Rittenhouse unlocked the door, but before he opened it he said, "Are you sure you want to do this, Mrs. Dennison?"

"I'm sure. Why are you trying to talk me out of it?"

"I'm not; I'm just . . ." A corner of his mouth twitched; he shook his head. "Five minutes, that's all the time I can spare."

It was cold inside the cabin, a little musty; Philip Dennison evidently hadn't bothered to air it out during his stay. The broken window's shutters were folded aside, but not enough daylight filtered in through the top half of the glass to give the room much clarity. Rittenhouse flipped a switch to light a pair of lamps. Mrs. Dennison went to the middle of the room, where she made a slow surveying turn.

There wasn't much to see. Native-stone fireplace, the broad hearth raised some six inches above a not quite even plank floor covered here and there by colored rag rugs. Long, high-backed couch facing the fireplace, a few other pieces of furniture. Knotty pine–paneled walls adorned with the kind of standard hunting and fishing prints favored by non-sportsmen. Kitchenette and dining nook at the rear, a short hallway separating them from bedroom and bathroom on the other side.

One of the rag rugs had been rolled up next to the fireplace. An effort had been made to sweep up the glass shards under the window, but small missed fragments glittered in the lamplight. Runyon glanced at the front door. Iron brackets were mounted on either side of it; the wooden crossbar, a plain redwood two-by-four, was propped against the wall below one of them.

Patricia Dennison said, "Where did you find him? In this room?"

Rittenhouse took off his hat. The band evidently irritated the patch of eczema; it looked redder and he rubbed at it. "Yes, ma'am."

"Where?"

"In front of the fireplace. He evidently slipped on the rug there, fell, and hit his head against the raised edge of the hearth." She started over there, and Rittenhouse said quickly, "I wouldn't look too closely, Mrs. Dennison —"

She ignored him, bending to peer along the stones. Runyon could see visible blood-stains where her husband had struck his head, but if she noticed them, and she must have, she didn't react. After a few seconds she straightened, eye-searched the room again.

"The bedroom?"

"Second door down the hall. I'm afraid it's still . . . well, it hasn't been tidied up."

"I don't care about that."

She went into the hallway, opened the bedroom door, and left it open after stepping through. Runyon didn't follow; neither did Rittenhouse.

"Mind if I ask how long Mr. Dennison had been dead before the body was discovered?" Runyon asked.

"Dr. Wolfe, our de facto coroner, estimates about twelve hours."

"Who found the body?"

"Next-door neighbor, the cabin we passed coming here. Year-round resident named Joe Meeker."

"Making a business or social call?"

"Business, I guess you'd say. Trying to drum it up. Joe's a handyman. Just back from a hunting trip and noticed some loose shingles on the roof, and when he saw Dennison's car he thought it might belong to the owner, Hansen. Knocked on the door, didn't get an answer, went around to the side, and saw the body when he looked through the window. He tried to get in and, when he couldn't, drove to the station and notified me right away."

"So he didn't know Dennison at all."

"Never met him."

"Did anyone else in Eagle Lake have any contact with him?"

"Just the glancing kind."

The answer struck Runyon as evasive. "He was here four days. He didn't spend all his time alone here, did he?"

"Went into the village to eat, buy groceries and liquor. Preferred his own company, I guess." Evasive again.

Patricia Dennison came out of the bedroom. She might have been a walking manikin — blank expression, nothing moving in her face, her eyes unblinking. "I'm ready to go now," she said.

They went out onto the porch and Rittenhouse relocked the door. On the way to the cruiser he said to her, "Excuse me for asking this, Mrs. Dennison, but . . . was it really worth it? Coming out here, looking around the cabin?"

Some kind of bird cut loose with a raucous cry from one of the trees. It was the only answer Rittenhouse got.

Back in the village, the deputy drove them to a newish hillside building bearing a sign that identified it as Eagle Lake Clinic. They weren't there long, either. Patricia Dennison formally identified her husband's body with one quick, dispassionate look and a nod and spent less than ten minutes making the arrangements with Dr. Wolfe for transportation of the remains to San Francisco.

At the substation Rittenhouse turned over an envelope containing Philip Dennison's personal effects, provided the name and location of the garage where his Caddy had been stored. His suitcase and other belongings were locked in the trunk, the deputy said. He asked Mrs. Dennison if she intended to spend the night in Eagle Lake or head back home this afternoon. It was late and she was too tired to start driving now, she said, she'd stay over and leave in the morning. He recommended the largest of the inns, the Eagle Lake Lodge, as having the most comfortable accommodations.

There were some papers to sign, and that was the end of it as far as Rittenhouse was concerned. Mrs. Dennison's behavior seemed to have disconcerted him; his relief that their business was finished was almost palpable. It wasn't finished, but he didn't know that yet.

Outside, as she and Runyon got into the Ford, she said in that abrupt way of hers, "Philip had a woman in that cabin, all right."

"Did you find something in the bedroom?"

"No."

"Then how can you be sure?"

"I could smell her in the bedroom, smell the sex."

After at least three days and nights? Runyon doubted that that was possible, unless she'd sniffed at the bedsheets. For all he knew that was what she'd done — she'd been alone in the bedroom long enough. In any event, he didn't argue with her.

"Before we go to the lodge," he said, "do I have permission to look through your husband's effects?"

She handed him the envelope without comment. Expensive Bulova Accutron wristwatch, Ray-Ban aviator sunglasses in a leather case, tooled leather wallet, keys, cell phone, pocketknife and nail clippers on a chain, some small change. The wallet, as he'd expected, contained nothing of interest: driver's license, half a dozen credit cards, sixty-three dollars in cash, a studio portrait of Mrs. Dennison. He put the wallet back into the envelope, removed the cell phone.

"I'd like to keep this for a while," he said, "return it to you later."

"You won't find the woman that easily.

Philip wouldn't have her number in his address book — he was too careful for that. And even if he did and you got hold of her, how would you know she was the one? She'd just deny it."

"Suppose you let me worry about that. All right to hang on to the phone?"

"Yes. Of course."

The chalet-style lodge was larger than it looked from a distance, two storied, with two elongated wings and landscaped grounds that included a large pond probably used for skating in the winter. Inside, the lobby and what Runyon could see of a big bar lounge appeared to be undergoing a transition from winter to summer hotel. A handful of staff members were in the process of altering decorations and moving furniture around. There were plenty of rooms available; Runyon and Mrs. Dennison each took one on the ground floor, but in different wings.

When they finished checking in, she asked him, "What are you going to do now?"

"The job you asked me to do, if I can."

She didn't ask him how he intended to proceed. All she said was, "Find her, whoever she is. Just find her."

Deputy Rittenhouse was away from the

substation again. He'd gone to the Lake-front Café just down the road, the dispatcher said. Runyon found him sitting alone in a blue leatherette booth, hunched over a piece of apple pie and a cup of coffee.

"Late lunch, Deputy?"

"That's right. Eat when you can in my work."

"Mine, too. Mind if I join you?"

Rittenhouse shrugged, made a sit-down gesture. Then, when Runyon slid in across from him, "Mrs. Dennison get settled all right?"

"Yes."

"What about you? You staying over, too?"

"At least for tonight."

"Why 'at least'?"

"I don't know yet how long it'll take to do the rest of my job."

"And just what would the rest of your job be?"

"Finding out why Philip Dennison came to Eagle Lake."

Rittenhouse started to say something, changed his mind, and forked a piece of pie into his mouth. A waitress came up while he was chewing — young, blond, chesty, with a bruise under one eye that a thick covering of makeup failed to hide. Runyon

79

ordered a grilled-cheese sandwich and hot tea. One of the deputy's eyebrows lifted at the tea order, but he made no comment.

Runyon said, "I think you might be able to help me. Don't take this the wrong way, but I got the impression you weren't completely forthcoming with Mrs. Dennison."

That got him a hard look, but it smoothed off after three or four beats. "Meaning what, exactly?"

"That maybe you have some idea of why her husband was here and wanted to spare her feelings."

The chief deputy finished his pie, pushed the plate away before he answered. "And you want me to tell you what that might be."

"I'm pretty good at what I do — I'll find it out anyway. But I'd rather hear it from you."

"And then go straight to Mrs. Dennison and tell her."

"Not necessarily. Depends on the information."

"Well, Christ. She really wants to know, even though it's going to hurt her?"

"Yes."

"All right, then," Rittenhouse said. "Dennison came here for a rendezvous with another woman. No surprise, huh?"

"No surprise. Who is she?"

"I don't know. Nobody knows. She didn't show up, at least not at the arranged time. Dennison was pretty pissed off. Did a fair amount of drinking at Eagle Lake Lodge and complained to the bartender about it."

"Not at the arranged time, you said. She came later?"

"May have. I can't say for sure."

"What makes you think she might have?"

Rittenhouse sighed. "Dennison wasn't alone at the cabin the entire time. Not unless he was into drunken self-gratification."

"That needs explaining."

"There were a couple of used condoms in the wastebasket in the bathroom. We bagged them up with the broken window glass and the rest of the trash. Nothing in any of that to point to the woman's identity." He started to rub his itchy scalp, stopped himself, and sighed again instead. "Good thing we did the bagging, or I wouldn't have let his wife go poking around the cabin like she wanted to."

He shouldn't have anyway. She hadn't needed to see used condoms to tell that some kind of sexual activity had gone on there.

"Anyhow," Rittenhouse said, "if the woman did show up, she was gone by the time Dennison slipped on that rug and bashed his head in. Maybe they had a fight and she walked out on him and that's why he got drunk. Anyhow, there wasn't anything at the cabin or in his vehicle to identify her."

Runyon's grilled cheese and tea arrived. Lipton's, not his favorite brand, but at least it was hot. He let the bag steep.

"Did Dennison say anything to the bartender at the inn about why she didn't show as arranged?" he asked.

"No. Just cursed women for being fickle and unpredictable."

"Give out any information about her, where she lived, how he knew her?"

"No." Rittenhouse paused and then said, "You might as well know the rest of it. This wasn't the first time Dennison's Sacramento buddy, Hansen, let him use the cabin."

"How many other times?"

"Three or four, according to Hansen. He said Dennison told him he was divorced, so he didn't see anything wrong in handing over the key."

Three or four. Patricia Dennison had alluded to two previous assignations. Could be there were others she didn't know about. "Different women or the same one? Hansen have any idea?"

"Not that he'd admit to."

"I'd like to talk to him. In person."

"And you want me to give you his phone number so you can set up a meeting."

"I'd appreciate it if you would. I'm a reputable investigator, Deputy. Check me out first if you like."

"I've already done that. After we got back to the substation."

Good law officer, Rittenhouse. Thorough. Good man, too; not every cop, small town or large city, cared enough to try to protect the feelings of a woman with a cheating husband.

"So can I have Hansen's phone number?"

"I'll give it to you when we're done here."

"And the name of the bartender at the lodge Dennison blabbed to?"

"Sam Granger. Works the four-till-closing shift."

"Okay if I use your name with him?"

"Go ahead." Rittenhouse watched Runyon take a bite of his grilled cheese, wash it down with a sip of tea. "Listen," he said then. "Are you going to tell your client what we just talked about? The condoms and the rest of it?"

"Not unless I find out who her husband came here to meet. That's her primary interest, the woman's name."

"She knows he was cheating on her, then?"

"She knows. This wasn't the first time."

"Figures. Then why is she so eager to know this woman's name?"

Runyon told him why.

"I don't know," Rittenhouse said, "that sounds kind of iffy to me. Borderline obsessive. You don't suppose she's got some kind of payback idea in her head?"

"Probably not the violent kind, but I don't know her well enough to be sure. I told her the only way I'd give her the woman's name was if I'm there when they meet."

"That's no guarantee she won't try something later."

"No, it isn't," Runyon admitted. "But at least it'd give me a better handle on her motives."

"Maybe you ought not to tell her at all. Or, better yet, drop your investigation completely."

"I can't do that without cause. Besides, as determined as she is, she'd just hire somebody else."

"Well, it's your call. But if anything bad does go down, it'll be on your conscience."

"Yeah," Runyon said, "I know it."

6

Fran Woodward was a self-employed designer of jewelry. Earrings, necklaces, bracelets made of gold, silver, and copper inset with beads and such and semiprecious gemstones. Had begun doing it in college at UC Berkeley and become so successful that her creations were featured in a variety of galleries and shops throughout the Bay Area, as well as sold at craft fairs and online through her website. She owned a house that doubled as her studio in Berkeley, not far from the university, and could be found there most days, including weekends. All of this courtesy of James Cahill and Tamara, who called with some preliminary background info as I was leaving Lafayette.

I probably should have gone to see Lieutenant Frank Kowalski, notify him that I had been hired by Cahill, but there was no urgency in that. Besides which, it was late afternoon by then and downtown Berkeley was more or less on my way back to San Francisco. I considered calling ahead to make sure Fran Woodward was at her studio, but it's always better not to give a potentially uncooperative individual advance notice. For all I knew, Kendra Nesbitt had contacted the designer after I left and warned her about me. Cahill had told me she was "mostly sympathetic" to him, but that didn't mean she would be receptive to an interview. It was worth the detour into Berkeley to find out if she was home and willing to talk.

Her address was less than three blocks off Telegraph Avenue, Berkeley's busiest and most multifarious street. At just about any hour except the middle of the night you'll find it jammed with humanity. Most are college students, but as in the Haight in San Francisco, there are also numerous street vendors dispensing all sorts of crafts, shoppers at the few remaining bookstores and other small businesses, curious and adventuresome tourists, homeless people pushing carts or curled up on the sidewalks, panhandlers, potheads, meth heads, cokeheads, and a transient criminal element. The good, the bad, the strange, the lost. There is a lot of energy on Telegraph, positive and negative. If you're smart, you walk the street with a cautious eye even in broad daylight.

Fran Woodward's home was an old tan-colored two-story frame job set back from the street, in good condition though it could use a fresh coat of paint. A cracked path led in to a narrow porch, at the foot of which was a discreet sign that had the word **Studio** and an arrow pointing to the left. I followed a continuation of the path around on that side, to a door with a window set next to it. The door was of heavy reinforced metal with a one-way glass peephole, and the window, blinded on the inside, had a set of security bars across it. Two more windows on the floor above were also barred. Security-conscious, Ms. Woodward, a wise choice for a woman engaged in a profitable business and living alone at least part of the time. Fran Woodward had never married, according to Tamara's research, instead maintaining a revolving-door relationship with a series of male companions.

Behind the door, some sort of electric tool was making a grinding noise. I waited until it stopped, then rattled my knuckles on the metal, there being no bell to push. Pretty soon I heard steps inside, but I got a long scrutiny through the peephole before a woman's voice, slightly annoyed, said, "Yes, what is it?"

"Ms. Woodward?"

"What do you want? I'm busy."

I told her my name and profession, holding my open license case up in front of the peephole to prove it. "I'd like to talk to you about Alice Cahill. I won't take up much of your time."

Six-beat. "Who are you working for?"

"James Cahill."

There was a little more silence; then a chain rattled and a dead bolt slid out of its casing and the door opened. Mrs. Cappicotti had described Fran Woodward as "kind of weird," dressing "like some sort of New Age hippie" and dyeing her hair odd colors. Right on. Her hair, cut fairly short, was shoe-polish black with lavender streaks, she wore a fringed orange tunic over a pair of patched jeans, she was barefoot, and she fairly bristled with jewelry. Earrings, a nose ring, bracelets, rings of various types and sizes on eight of her fingers and four of her toes. A walking advertisement for her craft. In one hand she held a small soldering iron.

"I don't know what happened to Alice," she said.

"Mr. Cahill says he has no idea, either. Do you believe him?"

Instead of answering the question, she invited me in with a wave of her hand that made the bracelets dance noisily. I went in past her, and she shut the door, put on the chain, then circled around me to the nearest of a pair of workbenches that covered two walls.

Some workshop. Organized chaos was the best description for it. Large, brightly lit, the room was packed with a variety of small hand and electric tools, some of which I could not identify; bins of beads and wood scraps and semiprecious stones; trays of silver and gold plate and copper; jars of hooks and rings and other kinds of fasteners; racks containing finished and partially finished jewelry items; hand-drawn designs on sheets of paper pushpinned to corkboards strung above the benches, and another design on a small artist's easel; and three different kinds of stools with padded seats. The smell of hot solder, metal, incense, and Ms. Woodward's musky perfume made for an uneasy mix that turned me into a temporary mouth breather.

She half-sat on one of the stools, her slender legs crossed at the ankles, the toe rings glinting in the light from overhead fluorescent tubes. "I believe him," she said, as if there hadn't been any elapsed time after my question. "I like Jimmy, despite his flaws. Always have."

"What sort of flaws?"

"You've met him, right? Kind of dorky in a sweet way." She waved a hand. "Sit down, why don't you. Take a load off."

Neither of the remaining stools looked as if they would hold my weight. I said, more or less truthfully, "Thanks, but I've been sitting most of the day. Dorky. I'm not sure what that means."

"Mild-mannered, passive. A small-balls guy."

Tamara would love that phrase. "Weak?"

"Not really, just never been able to get his shit together. Not that many men could, living with Alice. Actually, he was perfect for her."

"How do you mean?"

"He's a pleaser, she was a take-charge girl. Did things her way and usually got what she wanted. Ruled their roost."

"You used the past tense. Do you think she's no longer alive?"

"Jesus, I hope she is. We've been friends since college; I guess Jimmy told you that. But it's been a week now and not a word yet." Ms. Woodward didn't seem particularly upset, but then some people keep a tight lid on their emotions. If they have any in the first place.

"And you have no idea what might have

happened to her?"

"No. Only thing I can think of is some stranger kidnapped her. No way she walked out of that house on her own."

"Would she have let a stranger in when she was there alone?"

"She might if she was given a good reason."

"Did she tell you about the woman who accused her of plagiarism?"

"No. Not a word. She always confided in me about everything, but not that. She must've felt it was so ridiculous it wasn't worth mentioning."

"How did you find out?"

"Jimmy told me, the last time I talked to him, a couple of days ago. He didn't know, either, until he found her e-mail file."

"Would you say there's any validity to the claim?"

"Are you kidding? Hell, no." Ms. Woodward paused, frowning. "You don't suppose that woman did show up at her house?"

"Would Alice have let her in if she had?"

"Might have, in order to bitch-slap the hell out of her. That's what I would've done."

"When did you last see Alice?"

"A few days before she disappeared."

"How did she seem then? More upset,

more nervous, than usual?"

"A little. She wouldn't say what was bugging her. The plagiarism crap, maybe."

"Or trouble with her husband?"

"She never had any trouble with Jimmy."

"Not even when he was drinking heavily?"

"What? He's not a boozer. What gave you that idea?"

"He'd had a couple of drinks when I talked to him earlier today."

"Well, who can blame him, the pressure he's under? But normally, no, one is his limit."

"And alcohol doesn't make him aggressive?"

"*Nothing* makes Jimmy aggressive. He's just not built that way."

"Her sister says they fought all the time and she was afraid of him, especially when he'd been drinking."

Fran Woodward made a derisive snorting noise. "I wouldn't believe a word that bitch Kendra told me. No, they didn't fight all the time, and no, she wasn't afraid of him."

"She evidently believed he wanted her dead, that he once tried to strangle her."

"Strangle her? Jimmy? Bullshit."

"He said she misinterpreted an attempt at

an embrace and tried to brain him with a lamp."

"Well, then it must have been during one of her anxiety attacks. She was liable to do or say anything when she forgot to take her meds. She went off on me once over some trivial thing, I don't even remember what it was. Next time I saw her it was as if it never happened."

"Did she forget her meds often?"

"Now and then, when she got wrapped up in her writing."

I said, "I take it you don't much care for Kendra Nesbitt."

"Can't stand her. She's the one Alice fought with, not Jimmy. They knew how to push each other's buttons. One of those love-hate sibling relationships."

"What did they fight about?"

"Jimmy, mainly. Kendra doesn't like him, never did. Thought he was bad for Alice, that she ought to divorce him."

"But Alice didn't agree."

"No way. She didn't love him anymore, but she depended on him. And he needed her just as much."

"She told you she didn't love him anymore?"

"Not in so many words. Pretty obvious, though."

"How did Alice get along with her doctor?"

"Doctor? Oh, you mean Kendra's husband. Paul was Alice's doctor only by default. She wouldn't let anybody else examine her, prescribe her meds."

"So they got along well?"

"Oh, yes. Fine and dandy."

"What's your opinion of him?"

"Not my type. But he's good-looking and I'll bet he has a hell of a bedside manner." That came out through a brief smirk. "He's a whole lot easier to get along with than Kendra."

"There's something else Mrs. Nesbitt told me," I said. "She thinks my client is having an affair."

Fran Woodward looked startled, then clapped her hands together hard enough to set the bracelets clicking like castanets. "An affair? My God, that's a hoot."

"You don't believe it?"

"Not on Kendra's say-so. Who's the alleged woman?"

"One of his co-workers. Megan Sprague."

"Never heard of her. If it is true, which I doubt, how did Kendra find out?"

"She wouldn't say."

"Then she probably made it up to make Jimmy look even more guilty. She's the one who sicced the cops on him in the first place, you know."

"Would Alice have said anything to you if she'd found out he was having an affair?"

"Sure she would. I told you, she always confided in me about anything important."

"How would she have handled it? Confronted him? Or just kept quiet and let it go on?"

"Why would she let it go on?"

"You said she didn't love him anymore."

"That doesn't mean she'd want him screwing somebody else. Even though they weren't sleeping together anymore. Kendra told you about that, too, I'll bet."

I let that slide by without a response.

"As for Alice's sex life," Fran Woodward said with another of those slight smiles, "she knew how to pleasure herself."

"Uh-huh. So then she might have tolerated an affair."

"Not before, she wouldn't have."

"Before?"

"Before the accident, the agoraphobia. The way things were now, needing Jimmy the way she did . . . Oh, hell, who knows? Alice was capable of just about anything except leaving that house of theirs." She shoved up from the stool. "If you're out of questions, I need to get back to work."

"Just one more. What color and make is your car?"

She arched an eyebrow. "What does that have to do with anything? Oh, right . . . the car Jimmy's neighbor saw in their garage that afternoon. You're way off base if you think it was mine. I was with a customer from noon until after three. That Walnut Creek cop, Kowalski, already asked me about that."

"I'd still like to know."

"VW Bug, two years old. Bright red. Satisfied?"

No, I wasn't, not at all. But I said, "Yes. Thanks for your time, Ms. Woodward."

"Well, I hope you find out what happened to Alice — nobody else seems able to. If she is alive, all the better for Jimmy. Me, too, of course."

She walked me to the door, shook my hand with her beringed one. As soon as I was outside, she shut it and I heard the chain and then the dead bolt rattle into their slots.

The interview had raised more questions than it answered, supplied more conflicting information to be sorted through. Fran Woodward seemed less concerned about the welfare of her best friend than she was about that of Jimmy Cahill. A secret passion for him, despite the disparaging statements about his character? She'd exhibited as much shock as disbelief and scorn over his alleged affair with his co-worker. If she did have a thing for him, it gave her a motive for disposing of Alice Cahill. The fact that she drove a red VW meant nothing; larger cars, the kind you can use for transporting somebody dead or alive, can be rented or borrowed.

One thing I was pretty sure of. Fran Woodward had not been completely truthful with me; was hiding something, some knowledge, for reasons of her own. She was guilty of that, if nothing else.

7

JAKE RUNYON

The main lounge at the Eagle Lake Lodge was a huge room, with a circular bar in its center surrounded by high and low tables, overstuffed chairs and couches covered in red-and-gold patterned cloth. Two walls were of floor-to-ceiling glass, one offering a view of a now-barren ski slope and its shutdown ski lift, the other of distant mountain peaks with their snow-laden crests. A native-stone fireplace stretched the entire length of a third wall, a log fire blazing on the hearth. At this hour, shortly past four o'clock, only a handful of early drinkers were on hand.

Runyon took all of this in, in one sweeping glance, then filed it away in his memory bank and paid no more attention to any of it. He waded through thick carpeting to the bar. Two customers sat on high-backed stools at one end; behind the plank, an equal number of barmen wearing red-and-gold jackets were doing busywork. One of the bartenders was black, the other white. It was the black man who came over when Runyon sat down.

"Yes, sir. What can I get you?"

"Draft beer. Would you be Sam Granger?"

"I would. Don't believe I know you."

"Jake Runyon." He had his license case out; he laid it faceup on the bar top. "Deputy Rittenhouse gave me your name, said to tell you it's okay for you to answer some questions for me."

Granger was middle-aged, gray at the temples of his close-cropped hair, more gray salting his thick mustache. He'd worked at his trade a long time, Runyon judged, encountered all sorts of different people; nothing much would surprise him, or alter his professional demeanor. He looked at the license, looked at Runyon, nodded, and said, "I'll get your draft first. Any preference?"

"Your favorite will do fine."

Granger moved over to the line of spigots on the backbar, came back with a pint glass filled to the brim. He set it down on a coaster, swabbed the bar around it with a towel, and then straightened and stood as if at attention. Ex-military, probably, Runyon thought.

"You're here about the man found dead out at the lake, I expect," he said.

"Philip Dennison, yes. I'm representing his wife."

"Poor woman."

"In more ways than one."

Granger nodded. "She know what kind of man he was?"

"No illusions."

"Uh-huh. Well, I figured he was married the first time I set eyes on him. Told me he wasn't, no wedding ring, but you get so you can tell."

"He was here last Friday night, I understand."

"Came in about five. We weren't busy and he was the talkative sort. Said he was waiting for a lady friend, she'd be meeting him here any minute. Only she didn't show up."

"He mention her name?"

"Not that I recall. Drinks and faces I remember, names not so much."

"How long did he wait for her?"

"Until almost seven. Four Tanqueray martinis and getting madder with each one. Kept grumbling about women always being late, always making a man wait to get them into bed, that kind of talk. Tried calling her a couple of times on his cell phone, but he couldn't get a clear signal. He left after I told him he'd have better luck using a land-line."

Runyon took a sip of his beer. "Was that the last time you saw him?"

"No," Granger said. "He came back an hour or so later, sat down here at my station again. Angrier than before. Ordered another martini and started in mouthing off against women in general and his lady friend in particular because she'd stood him up."

"Did he say why she stood him up?"

"Something about all of a sudden changing her mind."

"How long did he stay that time?"

"Hour or so. Two more Tanquerays." Granger's mouth quirked slightly. "Muttered something like 'I'll show her' and then started in trying to work the room."

"Hitting on unattached women?"

"Trying to, like I said. There weren't many, not this time of year. Turndowns made him even madder. Asked me where a man could find some action in this damn dead backwater. His words."

"What was your answer?"

"The truth," Granger said, and let it go at that.

Runyon asked, "Did he leave then?"

"No. He wanted to know about a blond

waitress over at the Lakefront Café. He'd been in there earlier and she'd given him the eye, acted real friendly, let him know she got off work at nine. He figured her for a pushover — what did I think? I didn't tell him what I thought. If I had, it might've cost me my job."

"What did you tell him?"

"I told him she was married and her husband was big and jealous and mean as a badger. He just laughed. Cocksure, the way drunks on the make can get. Climbed off his stool and out he went."

"Did you see him any night after that?"

"No. Never came in while I was on shift."

Runyon was remembering the waitress who had served him and Rittenhouse at the Lakefront Café earlier. Blond, attractive, wearing makeup that didn't quite conceal the bruise under one eye. He said, "I have to ask this. If Dennison went to the café and hit on the waitress, would he have stood a chance with her?"

"I'd rather not say. Draw your own conclusions."

"Mind telling me her name?"

"Verna. Verna Meeker."

"Meeker. Any relation to the man who found Dennison's body, Joe Meeker?"

"Her husband," Granger said. "Only he's

not big. Thin as a rail, can't weigh more than one-fifty."

"Jealous, mean as a badger?"

"Jealous anyway."

"Would you say Dennison made a mistake if he did go after Verna Meeker?"

"I'd say any married man who goes after another man's wife is a damn fool."

Except for a handful of early-bird diners, the Lakefront Café was in a lull period. The blond waitress, Verna Meeker, was still on shift. Runyon sat in the same booth as before; the ones on either side were empty.

She came over to him, her movements slower than before, almost shuffling. Not so much tired from a long day on her feet, but as if she was stiff and hurting. He hadn't looked at her closely before; he did so now. The lines around her eyes and mouth said that her thirty-five years or so of living had not been easy ones. Some of the makeup covering the eye-shiner had worn off, so that you could see it more plainly, and her hair, more wheat colored than true blond, hung limp and lusterless over her uniform collar. Still, she was attractive in a hard and hungry sort of way.

He said, "Remember me? I was here earlier with Deputy Rittenhouse."

"I remember. Hot tea, wasn't it?"

"That's right."

"Anything else?"

"A few questions, if you don't mind."

Her mouth bent cynically. "Don't bother asking them. I'm not interested."

"Not those kinds of questions."

"Well, then?"

"They concern the man your husband found dead two days ago, Philip Dennison."

An emotion Runyon took to be fear flashed in her eyes, then vanished as though behind quick-drawn shutters. One hand came up toward her face, as if to touch the bruise — an involuntary gesture that she caught and arrested midway. "What about him?"

"Did you know him?"

"No."

"He came in here a few times, didn't he? Big, friendly guy. You must have waited on him."

"I'm not the only waitress works here."

"But you were working Friday night. He came in around eight-thirty or so, half in the bag on martinis. Remember him now?"

". . . All right, so I remember him. So what?"

"The woman he was supposed to meet

stood him up and he was looking for company."

"Yeah? Well, he didn't find it here."

"But you waited on him, talked to him?"

"Like any other customer. Like you."

"Did you see him again later?"

"What do you mean by that?" Sharp, defensive.

"He was in Eagle Lake three more days. The cabin he was staying in is right down the road from where you live."

She leaned forward, so low and close that the thrust of her large breasts nearly touched his arm. "What the hell you trying to say, mister?"

"Just asking if you saw the man again."

"So what if I did? It's none of your business."

"Not mine — his wife's."

"What's his wife have to do with it?"

"She wants to know what he did the four days he was in Eagle Lake, why he stayed here when the woman he was waiting to meet stood him up. He was supposed to be in L.A."

"How should I know what he did? I don't know and I don't care."

"Don't care that he's dead?"

"I didn't know him; why should I?"

She straightened, pivoted away from the

booth. When she came back with the tea, she wouldn't make eye contact. She slapped the cup down hard enough to spill some of it on the table, went away again fast.

Runyon neither drank the tea nor mopped up the spill. He put two dollars on the table and left the café. No need to linger; he'd found out what he'd gone there for.

The Meeker cabin sat on high ground across the road from the lake. On one side of it, a section of forest had been cleared to make room for two outbuildings — one of them large, the size of a small barn, which probably served Joe Meeker as a workshop, the other a shed for storage of winter firewood. There were no vehicles in sight when Runyon drove by. No smoke from the cabin's chimney, either, or any other signs of life.

Since he was close to the Hansen cabin, he figured he might as well have another look around the property. But it wasn't deserted as he'd expected. A dark green Chevy Silverado pickup with a contractor's service body of racks and bins fitted onto its bed was parked in the meadow below the cabin. Joe Meeker's vehicle, evidently. The plywood sheet had been removed from the side-wall window and a short blade of a man was in the process of installing a new pane of glass. He stopped what he was doing when Runyon drove in, stood watching him park and then cross the pine-needled ground.

Meeker was somewhere around forty, the owner of a narrow, bony face and the small, bright eyes of a lizard. Long, shaggy brown hair was pulled back on his scalp and rubber-banded into a ponytail. Despite his thinness, there appeared to be a lot of muscular gristle in him. A tool belt circled his narrow waist and he held a putty knife in one knobby hand.

"Who're you?" he demanded.

Runyon told him. And got a slitty look in return.

"Detective? What's Dennison's wife want with a detective? His death was an accident; he was drunk and he slipped and fell. There's no doubt about that. Cabin was all locked up."

"I wasn't hired to investigate the man's death."

"No? What for, then?"

Runyon repeated what he'd told Meeker's wife at the café.

"You're wasting your time," the handyman said. "Dennison didn't have any woman with him while he was here."

"You know that for sure? I understand you were away all weekend on a hunting trip."

"Who told you that?"

"Deputy Rittenhouse happened to mention it."

"Yeah, well, that's right. Wasn't worth the trip. One small buck and I had to share the meat with my two buddies."

"When did you leave?"

The question produced a frown. "What's it to you?"

"I was just wondering if you saw Philip Dennison before you left."

"No, I didn't see him. Left early Friday morning, got back late Monday night. Never laid eyes on him until I come by Tuesday morning and spotted his body through this window."

"Never? He'd been up here a couple of times before. With a woman each time, apparently."

"I don't know nothing about that. He was a stranger to me." Meeker gestured with the putty knife. "Listen, I got permission from the owner to be here, fix this window. He give you permission to come snooping around? Or did Rittenhouse?"

"No."

"Then what're you doing here? There's nothing for you to see. Maybe you better just leave, let me finish my work."

Runyon shrugged. "Maybe so."

He walked to the Ford, backed it around. As he was pulling up onto the road, he glanced in the side-view mirror. Meeker was still standing in the same spot, looking after him, his bony features drawn into a frown.

In his room at the lodge Runyon went through the address book on Philip Dennison's cell phone. There were more than forty numbers that ranged over much of California, some with the names of companies, some with full or partial names, some with initials, a few with no identification of any kind. All of the full or partial names were male. He copied down those with initials only and those without ID, a total of fourteen. The lodge was equipped with high-speed Wi-Fi; he hooked up his laptop and transferred the list of fourteen numbers into an e-mail to Tamara at the agency, along with a request for as many names and addresses as she could locate.

While he was at it, he made one other request — for background information on Patricia Dennison. He was still leery of her interest in her husband's mistress, her desire to confront the woman. The more he knew about Mrs. Dennison, the better able he'd be to understand what motivated her and what her intentions might be. And how to handle the situation if he did manage to uncover the girlfriend's identity.

A number in Philip Dennison's address book labeled **Lloyd** was the same as the one Rittenhouse had given him for Lloyd Hansen's insurance agency in Sacramento. He called it and was told that Hansen had already left for home. Runyon talked the woman he spoke to into letting him have the home number.

Hansen sounded wary and flustered when he came on the line. And not very convincing when he said, "I already told the deputy up there, Rittenhouse, everything I know about Phil Dennison."

"I'd appreciate hearing it from you in person. I could drive down to Sacramento tomorrow, any time that's convenient for you."

". . . Well, as a matter of fact, I'm planning to drive up there in the morning. Check on the cabin. The handyman, Meeker, is supposed to fix the broken window —"

"He already did."

"Good. But I still want to have a look at the place, clean it up. I don't suppose the sheriff's people did that."

"What time do you expect to get here?"

"Sometime around noon, probably."

"I could meet you at the cabin," Runyon said, "and we could talk there. I won't take up much of your time."

"I guess that'd be okay."

Unless Patricia Dennison contacted him tonight, tomorrow morning before she left for San Francisco was soon enough to speak to her again. It wouldn't be much of a conversation in any case. He had nothing to report to her yet; suspicions weren't facts. For that matter, even if he was able to verify that Philip Dennison and Verna Meeker had had relations he was not at all sure he would tell her about it. Did she really need to know about, much less have words with, a local tramp Dennison had picked up on the drunken rebound? He didn't think so.

He lay down on the bed, used the remote to put on the TV for noise. Later, when he felt hungry enough, he'd go out somewhere to eat. But it wouldn't be to the Lakefront Café.

8

TAMARA

She was thinking again about Horace's marriage proposal when the surprise call came in to the agency.

The call had nothing to do with Horace or the proposal. It was 4:30 and she was once again taking a break from her work, sitting tipped back in her desk chair, her fourth or fifth cup of coffee of the day in hand. The coffee didn't do anything for her except make her have to pee, but it was as good an excuse as any to get up and fuss around when her attention started to wander from the business at hand, as it had been doing most of the day.

"Marry me, Tam." Just like that, out of the blue . . . well, out of the semidarkness of her bedroom last night after they'd finished making sweaty love. No warning of any kind, wham. If words could knock you down, she'd have been out of bed and lying dizzy on the floor.

"You're kidding, right?" she'd said.

And he'd said, "I've never been more serious. I love you and you love me; it's about time we made this arrangement permanent. What do you say?"

Well, what *could* she say? You're crazy, bro, and I'd be crazy to say yes? You big ugly bastard, you walked out on me for that two-year gig with the Philadelphia symphony, broke my heart when you moved in with Mary from Rochester after promising you'd always be faithful to me, and then when both the gig and the affair busted up you come crawling back to San Francisco and sweet-talk me into bed again. Things haven't been all rosy since, either. Together again, not together for a while, back together again; work too hard, sleep and eat too little because I'm off my feed. And now all of a sudden you expect me to let you put a ring on my finger and another one through my nose. You really think I'm so hot for you and that dumbstick of yours I'll forget about the past and go traipsing off into a future full of who knows what?

Maybe I am.

Damn you, Horace Fields, maybe I am.

She tried again to imagine what it would be like having him around all the time instead of two or three nights a week and a weekend now and then; to come home to him from the agency every night, completely change her comfortable, do-what-she-liked-when-she-liked lifestyle. Sure, they'd lived together before he went off to Philly, but they'd been a lot younger then, her studying computer tech at S.F. State and then going to work for Bill, Horace studying cello at the conservatory. Good times with no real commitment. And he hadn't been easy to live with, always on her case about her prickly family relationships and her "low-life friends" and not keeping the apartment as neat and clean as he liked it.

Now they weren't just years older; they were different people, different kinds of opposites. Back then she'd been an angry, know-it-all, grunge-dressing wiseass; he'd been dedicated and tolerant and mostly together. Positions reversed now. She was the responsible one, the focused one, running a business she'd helped build up from a one-man operation into one of the more successful private agencies in the city, putting in long hours by choice and loving it; he was just drifting, working at a teaching job he didn't much like, playing his cello on a catch-as-catch-can basis with a freelance chamber music group, worrying that he wasn't good enough or lucky enough to ever get another symphony seat.

All the makings of a big mistake, Tamara. Man's not about to change and neither are you. Are you really ready to give up your freedom for Horace, no matter how much you think you might still love him? Be tied to him for the rest of your life, or however long the marriage might last?

Love. What is love, anyway? A whole lot more than just sex, that's for sure, no matter how good the sex is. It's caring and overcoming adversity and being there for each other, no matter what. It's the kind of marriage Mom and Pop have had for nearly forty years, that Kerry and Bill have. You'd always be there for Horace because that's the kind of woman you are now, but would he always be there for you? Like if something really bad happened, a disease or an accident or some new on-the-job crisis, God forbid. Or would he man-down instead of man-up and just slip and slide away?

That Mary from Rochester . . . one minute they were so hot for each other they were planning to get married; then all of a sudden they were quits. He claimed it was because he realized he was still in love with his old sweetie Tamara and that was why he called it off with Mary. But was that the truth? Or had Mary dumped him when he lost his seat with the Philly symphony and the only reason he'd come back to S.F. was because he couldn't find another gig or another woman who'd have him back there?

Could she really trust him? Screwed her over once, he could do it again. Couldn't trust her feelings, either, for that matter. Men she'd cared for had been screwing her over most of her life. Dudes back in her grunge days, Horace, then that son of a bitch Lucas Delman . . . she'd trusted Lucas, thought she might be falling for him, and look what'd happened there. She was lucky to be alive after *that* monster mistake.

But Horace wasn't Lucas, dammit. He had his good points — he was gentle, he was affectionate, he was honest (well, mostly honest), he insisted on working and paying his own way. And he genuinely cared for her or he wouldn't have made the proposal. "I love you, Tam, I've always loved you." Could've been bullshit, but she didn't think so. But did he know what love really was any more than she did? The proposal had come right after they'd hotted up the sheets for more than an hour. Could've had more to do with that than been a genuine expression of his feelings, couldn't it?

Back and forth, back and forth.

She needed time to think, weigh all the positives and negatives, before she made up her mind and gave him her answer. She'd told him that and he'd said, "Don't take too long, baby," and then he'd laughed and added, "I might change my mind and withdraw the offer."

Not funny, Horace. Nothing to joke about. Serious business, man, real serious business . . .

The ringing phone jerked her out of her reverie. Not her cell, the agency landline. She set down the cup of cold coffee, lifted the receiver, gave the standard agency greeting.

Couple of seconds of staticky silence. Then a man's voice, young and so low-pitched she could barely make out the words, said, "I want to speak to Jake Runyon."

"He's not here. Can I take a message?"

"Will he be in today?"

"No, I'm sorry, he's away on business."

"Away from the city? From the Bay Area?"

Tamara frowned. There was an odd sort of inflection in the young voice, a kind of tension. "I can't give out that information. Who's calling, please?"

"When do you expect him back?"

"Not until Monday."

"Where can I reach him? I had his card with his cell and home numbers, but I misplaced it."

"You know Mr. Runyon, have business with him?"

"I know him."

"I asked if you have business with him."

"Yes. Business."

"What kind of business?"

"Personal. What's his cell number?"

"You're just a voice to me," Tamara said, losing patience. "Who are you and why do you want to speak to Mr. Runyon?"

Silence. She was on the point of breaking the connection when he said, "Never mind. There's really no point in talking to him if he's away somewhere. I can wait until next week. Monday's soon enough." Another pause. Then, abruptly, "Will you be speaking to him before then?"

"I don't know. Possibly."

"If you do, don't tell him I called."

"Don't tell him *who* called?"

"Joshua Fleming."

And the line went dead.

Tamara sat holding the receiver. Joshua Fleming. Jake's son, his estranged gay son. The reason Jake had moved down from Seattle after his second wife died, to try to end a twenty-year estrangement, re-establish a relationship. Total failure. Even after Joshua's lover was gay-bashed in the Castro and Jake had nailed the homophobes responsible, the dude still wouldn't have anything to do with him. Poisoned against him while he was growing up by his mother, Jake's first wife, a bitter, grudge-holding drunk — the kind of poison that gets worked in so deep you can't flush it out. It'd been, what, four years now since that gay-bashing business? Yeah, four years, because it'd happened around the same time she'd made her one and only attempt at doing fieldwork and got herself kidnapped and nearly killed.

As far as she knew, Jake had given up trying to reconcile with his son after that, had had no contact of any kind with him since. Now, out of the blue, this phone call. Why? Some new investigation Joshua wanted him to take on? Or had Joshua had a change of heart for some reason, decided it was finally time to end the estrangement?

She really hoped that was it. A reconciliation would mean more to Jake than anything else.

9

A lot of years have passed since the '89 Loma Prieta earthquake, but whenever I have occasion to drive cross the Bay Bridge I still have a memory tweak and a vague frisson of unease to go with it. Too much imagination, too much empathy. All the destruction when the section of the upper deck collapsed into the lower, the panic, the casualties.

The bridge has undergone numerous repairs, alterations, retrofitting in the years since, including a complete replacement of the span's eastern leg, yet construction and other problems continue to plague it and cause engineers to question its seismic safety — saltwater intrusion into the tower's foundation, damage to its anchor rods, substandard deck welds, water leaks near rods that secure the main cable, weak spots in the concrete wall in the Yerba Buena tunnel mid-span. If I believed in jinxes and curses, I might consider the bridge to be doomed. As it is, particularly headed westbound at approximately the same time of day as the quake struck, 5:04 P.M., I can't help feeling a sliver of relief when I finally exit.

When Tamara called, I was stuck in a long line of cars waiting to get through the toll plaza. The evening rush-hour traffic is twice as heavy eastbound, since large numbers of people who work in the city live in the East Bay, but there's no toll in that direction, and the westward flow is substantial enough to cause the plaza backup even with the Fas-Trak lanes. So her call was well-timed because it took my mind off the upcoming crossing.

She asked me where I was and I told her. "Going where?" she asked. "Back here to the office?"

"Hadn't planned on it, no."

"Wondering because I'm about to ready to leave."

"Early night for you. Hot date?"

"Hot bath, alone. How'd your interviews go?"

"Not too well. Conflicting stories from Cahill, Kendra Nesbitt, and Fran Woodward. I'll talk to the client again tomorrow, try to sort them out."

"You thinking of seeing the Dellbrook woman tonight?"

"No. I want to compare her romance book to the one she claims Alice Cahill plagiarized before I talk to her."

"Bet you're looking forward to that."

"Oh, yeah. You wouldn't want to do the reading for me, would you?"

"Fat chance. Only thing I'm taking into my bath is a glass of vino."

"Uh-huh. You turn up anything on her I should know?"

"One thing. She doesn't own a car or have a driver's license, just a state ID card."

Usually that meant the person didn't drive. But not necessarily that they didn't know how to drive or hadn't driven before, or wouldn't again in a borrowed car if they considered it necessary. By itself the fact didn't eliminate Grace Dellbrook as a suspect.

"Where does she live, work?"

"Lives alone in a studio apartment at 2930 Larkin, works as a teller at the Chase branch near Civic Center. Fifty-four, divorced, one grown daughter living in Michigan. No criminal record of any kind."

"What about the accident victim, Sofia Hernandez?"

"Squeaky clean like Dellbrook and the

rest. Nurse at a health-care facility for the elderly in Pleasant Hill. Still lives there. Divorced ten years; two grown kids, one in college, the other working for an electrical contractor. That one got into some trouble with the law when he was seventeen — swiped and vandalized a car — but that was before the accident. No law trouble since."

"Okay. I'll talk to her if nothing else turns up. But after the insurance settlement and four silent years, she doesn't figure to be involved." The cars ahead of me were moving along at slightly more than a snail's pace now. Almost to the line of toll booths. "Couple of things you can do for me, but they can wait until tomorrow. Mrs. Nesbitt told me the Cahills have a hundred-thousand-dollar joint life insurance policy with Statewide Mutual. See if you can find out if the policy is still in force."

"Will do," Tamara said. "What else?"

"Cahill allegedly has a girlfriend, a woman named Megan Sprague who works with him at Streeter Manufacturing. Background on her, and anything you can pick up on the alleged affair."

"Megan Sprague, Streeter Manufacturing. Right."

Still inching. Come *on*, I thought, let me onto and across the damn bridge so I can come back and run the eight-mile gantlet twice more tomorrow.

Tamara said, "Oh, one thing before I let you go. I had a kind of funny call on the agency line a few minutes ago."

"From?"

"Jake's son, Joshua, wanting to talk to him."

That raised an eyebrow. "You mean they're back in touch after, what, more than three years? Jake didn't say anything to me —"

"No, I don't think so. He sounded . . . I don't know, wired up tight, like he was upset about something. He wanted to know when Jake'd be back after I said he was away on business. Then he asked for Jake's cell number — said he'd lost Jake's card."

"You give him the number?"

"No. I would have, but he wouldn't tell me his name until right before he hung up. Before that he said never mind, he could wait until next week, Monday was soon enough. And don't tell Jake he called."

"Keeping it private between them," I said, "direct contact only. Best if we stay out of it anyway. Jake'll tell us if he wants us to know."

Through the FasTrak in my lane, finally, and into the flow of traffic on the bridge. I

124

ended the conversation with Tamara and concentrated on my driving.

My home life is good these days. For too long a time it had been unsettled, at times terrifying and extremely painful — Kerry's breast cancer scare, the physical and psychological torment she had been subjected to in Green Valley, the death of her mother, Cybil. But Kerry had weathered and come to terms with it all, with Emily's and my support, and the times of crises had brought the three of us even closer together.

The one thing that still worried me, admittedly without any real justification, was Emily's budding womanhood. She was fifteen now and *una bellezza delle bellezze* — a dark-haired, dark-eyed, sweet-faced beauty of beauties. Boys swarmed around her like flies to honey, not just those her age but the older, more testosterone-driven types as well. Kerry wasn't concerned at all; she'd long since had The Talk with her and had every faith in Emily's intelligence (smart as a whip, A student in all subjects) and in her promise not to let herself be taken advantage of (she'd never yet broken a promise). Besides which, Emily was fine with the rule we'd set that she was not allowed unsupervised dates until after her sixteenth birthday.

And there was no one particular boy she was attracted to . . . yet.

Still, I worried. For a couple of reasons: I'd become an adoptive father late in life and was inclined to be overprotective as a result, and I was not too old to remember the power of raging teenage hormones. I had been a pretty clean-cut kid, in deference to my mother, a devout Catholic lady; she'd had a hard life, putting up with my drunken, abusive old man, and I felt protective toward her, too, hadn't wanted to give her any more pain. Even so, my raging hormones had run wild on a couple of occasions, one of which almost made me an unwilling parent myself at age seventeen. That wouldn't happen to Emily; of course it wouldn't. But I could not help thinking of how many thousands of fathers had been unshakably and incorrectly convinced it wouldn't happen to their daughters. . . .

Emily was in the midst of an impromptu concert, singing unaccompanied to an audience of one, Kerry, when I got home. I could hear Emily even before I unlocked the condo door, so I went in quiet, set the Alice Cahill–Grace Dellbrook e-mail file on the hallway table, and stood there listening. The song was one I hadn't heard before, didn't recognize, but it was an understandable choice given the sudden tragic loss of both her parents and the revelation of their hidden criminal past — a haunting piece about loneliness. She had a sweet, clear voice, the kind sometimes described as angelic, and justifiably so in her case. Her heart was set on a singing career — she sang in school productions and was taking private lessons from an established professional who encouraged her. That was another good reason why I should not have been concerned about her personal conduct. She would never do anything to jeopardize her future plans.

You know something, pal? I said to myself while I listened. You're a damned old fuddy-duddy. What you should be fretting about is whether or not you'll live long enough to hear your daughter perform onstage, on TV, somewhere in front of a large audience of people who won't be one-tenth as proud of her as you.

When she finished her song, I went into the living room clapping lustily. Kerry joined in, and Emily beamed and bowed and then came over to give me a hug. Special little family moment. The song, it turned out, was one by Taylor Swift called "A Place in This World." If Ms. Swift had heard Emily's rendition, she surely would have applauded, too.

Kerry was in good spirits. She'd heard from the small-press publisher that was doing e-book and print-on-demand paperback editions of her mother's collected works — three volumes of novelettes from various forties pulp magazines and the two full-length novels written more recently, *Dead Eye* and *Black Eye,* all of which featured private detective Max Ruffe. They had originally appeared under the pseudonym Samuel Leatherman, but the reissues would be published with the byline "Cybil Wade writing as Samuel Leatherman," with introductory memoirs written by Kerry. A fitting tribute to a much-loved woman of considerable talent.

"They've gotten some very nice quotes from contemporary writers that should help with sales," Kerry told me. When she was happy like this, there was a glow in her eyes and on her face that made her look ten years younger. Still and forever another *bellezza delle bellezze,* whether her hair was her natural auburn or turned gray or pure white. "The books will be available next week. Copies of the paperback edition are on the way, should be here tomorrow or Monday. I can't wait to see them."

"Likewise. The pulp-style covers look great."

"Cybil would've been pleased. Though she'd have insisted it was all a big fuss over nothing. She never did hold her work in very high regard."

"No," I said, "but I think maybe we convinced her she was a much better writer than she gave herself credit for."

"Better than most of her male counterparts in the pulp era."

"Ninety-eight percent of them. I must've read more than two thousand pulp stories over the years. If that doesn't qualify me as an expert judge, I don't know what would."

"She was a wonderful writer," Emily said. "I didn't think I'd like reading her stories in those old magazines, but I did. Her novels, too."

I know a good cue when I hear one. "Speaking of novels," I said, "how would you ladies like to help me with some literary detective work if you're not busy tonight?"

"What sort of literary detective work, Dad?"

"Reading and comparing a couple of novels."

"Mysteries?"

"No. Romance novels."

Kerry said, "You don't mean the fat, sexy kind?"

"No. The, ah, short, sappy kind."

"You're not kidding, are you."

"Nope." I hauled the paperbacks of *What the Bride Found Out* and *The Convenient Bride* out of my coat pocket, extended them one in each hand. "I'm no judge of this type of fiction — I doubt I could get through both of them by myself tonight — and I'd like the female perspective."

"Why do you want them compared?"

I explained about the new client and his missing wife, the plagiarism accusation, the e-mails from Grace Dellbrook that outlined the alleged theft points. "Before I see the Dellbrook woman tomorrow, I need a better idea of whether or not there's any validity to the claim. But if you're both too busy with other things . . ."

"I'm not," Emily said. "Mom? I'm a fast reader and so are you. It wouldn't take all that long for each of us to read both."

"And then compare our notes to the detailed similarities in the e-mails." The idea appealed to Kerry, too. "All right," she said to me, "but Emily and I don't work for free. It'll cost you a restaurant meal and a movie this weekend."

"Deal."

We had a light supper and then got to it, Emily curled up on the living room couch with Shameless the cat in her lap, Kerry and me in our Barcaloungers. While each of them read one of the novels, both turning pages at a rapid clip, I went over the e-mail exchanges again, then the background specifics on Grace Dellbrook Tamara had forwarded. Kerry and Emily finished reading at about the same time, then swapped books. This go-round took longer because they paused now and then to make notes. It was almost ten o'clock by the time they finished. The comparison of their notes, and then the notes with the e-mails, took another half hour.

Result: Complete agreement with Grace Dellbrook on the various points of similarity she'd raised, plus three additional points both Kerry and Emily had found and a fourth on Kerry's list. Plot, character, scene setting, descriptive passages lifted from the clumsily written *What the Bride Found Out* and smoothly rewritten in *The Convenient Bride.*

"No doubt about it," Kerry said. "Alice Cahill, alias Jennifer West, is a thief. How many books did you say she'd written?"

"A dozen or so, according to her husband," I said.

"Makes you wonder, doesn't it, how many of those might also have been stolen?"

10

Before I left the condo on Friday morning, I called the Van Ness Avenue branch of Chase Bank and asked to speak to Grace Dellbrook. She was there — it was shortly after their 9:00 A.M. opening — and when she came on the line I gave my name and profession, asked if I could meet with her to discuss an important matter.

Her response took some time coming. "What important matter? What does a detective want with me?"

"I'd prefer to discuss it in person, Ms. Dellbrook. Could we meet somewhere, a public place, during your lunch hour?"

More dead air. "No, not unless you give me some idea of what this is about."

"It concerns Alice Cahill."

I took the sound I heard on the line to be that of a quick-drawn breath. Then, "She hasn't changed her mind, has she?"

"Changed her mind about what?"

"The money."

"I know nothing about any money."

". . . Are you working for her?"

"No, ma'am, I'm not."

"Who then? What's this about?"

"Mrs. Cahill and the fact that she's missing."

"Missing? My God . . ."

"I really think we should talk, Ms. Dellbrook, as soon as possible. Is there someplace public we can meet during your lunch break?"

I waited through another period of dead air. "All right," she said finally. "There's a Starbucks not far from the bank."

"Fine. What time?"

"I can be there a little after twelve. How will I know you?"

I described myself and the suit and tie I was wearing. Retirement age and hardly a menacing figure. She said, "All right," again and broke the connection.

Next call: James Cahill's home number. No answer, no machine pickup. I tried his cell and the call went straight to voice mail. So then I rang up Streeter Manufacturing. He was there, but in a meeting that was expected to last for some time. I left an ASAP callback message for him.

Third and final call: Prime Medical Group

in Walnut Creek, a consortium of doctors that included Paul Nesbitt. I did not expect to get through to him and I didn't. If he was anything like his wife, he wouldn't want anything to do with me, but I left a request for a callback anyway.

I drove down to South Park. The $2.8 million renovation project that had begun late in 2015 was complete now — thirty or so dead or dying trees removed and twenty-four new mature ones planted, an expanded children's play area, new ADA accessible curb ramps at each of the park's four entry points. Deconstruction and construction noise had been constant and intrusive for what seemed like an endless period of time, but what can you do when your offices are located in a building facing a prime-location park, the rent is still affordable even with recent increases, and office space elsewhere in the heart of the city is both hard to come by and exorbitantly expensive these days? You tolerate the inconvenience, naturally, and become so used to it after a while that you're able to tune much of it out. The agency, now that all the renovation was done, seemed almost too quiet to Tamara. Not to me. There can't be enough quiet to suit me in this racket-filled world.

Tamara has a number of different personas, depending on her mood and the state of things in her personal life. Practical. Playful. Grouchy. Pensive. Cool. Bawdy. Talkative. Withdrawn. Others, too. What I walked in on today was Pensive Tamara. That meant, according to past experience, that there was something weighing on her mind that she was trying to work out or come to terms with. Something to do with Horace Fields and their iffy relationship, probably. I knew better than to ask her. If she wanted to talk about it, she would. And today she didn't.

One thing she was, always, was efficient, attentive, and sharp when it came to business. I told her what Kerry and Emily and I had determined about Alice Cahill, and the first thing she said paraphrased Kerry's words of last night: "If she did it once, it probably wasn't the only time. Serial book thief."

"In which case she was bound to get caught sooner or later," I said. "Grace Dellbrook was apparently the first victim to tumble. No other such correspondence in her files, or Cahill would have mentioned it."

"Unless she didn't keep a record of any other accusations, or did and destroyed the evidence."

"Possible, but then why keep the Dellbrook file?"

"Yeah. Not an honest person, in any case. Agoraphobia's no excuse."

"Agreed."

"You think her husband knows?"

"I doubt it. She wouldn't have told him, and she wasn't worried about him snooping in her files. They had a privacy pact, and he's the . . . deferential type." I almost used Fran Woodward's phrase: *small-balls guy.*

"You going to tell him?"

"I don't know yet," I said. "Depends on if it has a bearing on her disappearance. I should have a better idea of whether or not Grace Dellbrook had anything to do with it after I talk to her."

The ringtone on my cellular is supposedly the most nonintrusive and melodious, but to me it sounds like some sort of bird warbling. The call that came in just then was from a woman at Prime Medical Group in Walnut Creek, who said that she was calling on behalf of Dr. Nesbitt. Would I be able to come in at three o'clock this afternoon for a brief consultation? Nesbitt evidently didn't share his wife's open hostility toward James Cahill and was inclined to be cooperative, at least up to a point. It had to be at his convenience and in his bailiwick,

137

however. Okay with me; I expected to head back to the East Bay again anyway after the meeting with Grace Dellbrook, for another face-to-face talk with the client. I said yes, Dr. Nesbitt could expect me at the appointed time.

Tamara finished up a background search that Jake Runyon had requested by e-mail from Eagle Lake, then pulled up the information I'd asked her for yesterday. James Cahill's alleged girlfriend, Megan Sprague, was thirty-one and a graduate of Cal State Santa Cruz with a degree in business administration. Employed in the marketing department at Streeter Manufacturing for four years. Married five years, divorced three — divorce amicable, not messy. Joint custody with her ex-husband of a six-year-old daughter, the child mostly residing with her and her aunt in Concord. No police record of any kind. No hint of any scandalous behavior, sexual or otherwise.

"Nothing much there," Tamara said. "If the client is sleeping with her, you think the relationship's justified?"

"Not my place to make moral judgments."

"Well, right or wrong, she doesn't seem to be the femme fatale type."

"On the surface, anyway. Background data can be misleading."

The joint insurance policy the Cahills had with Statewide Mutual was still in effect, a standard one-hundred-thousand-dollar term life that had been taken out at the time of their marriage and on which not a single premium had been missed. There were no contingent beneficiaries. Dead end there, I was fairly sure, whether Kendra Nesbitt thought so or not.

Just before I left the agency at 11:30, James Cahill returned my call. Full of apologies, as though he'd done something wrong by spending most of the morning in a business meeting. Streeter Manufacturing was located in Concord, the city adjacent to Walnut Creek on the north; I preferred to see him there, in case I found it necessary to talk to Megan Sprague as well, and the consultation with Dr. Nesbitt probably wouldn't take more than a few minutes. I arranged to meet with Cahill in his office between 4:00 and 4:15.

The Chase branch at Van Ness and McAllister is close to City Hall and the Civic Center Plaza, and street parking is highly problematical in the area despite the city's exorbitant meter rates. Parking in the Civic Center Garage beneath the Plaza is even pricier, but since it was an expense account item I left my car in there and walked over to the specified Starbucks.

One of the many things that puzzle me about today's world is the coffee culture perpetuated by Starbucks, Peet's, and similar establishments. I drink a fair amount of coffee at home and the office, and espresso sometimes after meals, but I like it plain and black; all these designer blends and concoctions — lattes, cappuccinos, macchiatos, Frappuccinos — do nothing for me. Nor does the idea of having a social life contingent upon the daily consumption of caffeine and caffeine drinks. Today's specials at this Starbucks were caramel brulée latte and chestnut praline latte. Fine if your taste runs to that sort of drink, I guess, but to me they were the liquid equivalent of topping rounds of bread dough with such as bananas, pineapple, arugula, artichokes, macadamia nuts, and artisan cheeses and calling them pizzas. No Italian in his right mind would make, let alone eat, a banana and goat cheese "pizza."

The place was jammed with noon-hour customers. All the tables were taken and there was a line at the counter. I stood around long enough to be recognized if Grace Dellbrook was one of the women in the crowd, then went outside and took up space near the entrance. I'd been there about five minutes when a large, fiftyish woman in a gray coat appeared, eyed me, and then approached and made a question of my name. When I acknowledged it, she asked to see identification; I obliged with the license photostat. Cautious lady, not that I blamed her.

"Pretty crowded inside, I'm afraid," I said. "We can wait for a table, if you like."

"No, I only have an hour for lunch." She seemed less nervous now. "If you don't mind waiting, I'll get a latte and a muffin and then we can go over and talk in the Plaza."

"Not a problem."

". . . Would you like me to get you something?"

I thought of the advertised latte specials. "No, but thanks for offering."

She was in and back out in six or seven minutes, carrying a paper sack. Ms. Dellbrook had nothing to say on the brisk walk over to the Plaza, her eyes straight ahead all the way. Okay with me. The kind of conversation we were about to have is better done in stationary positions.

The Plaza is a typical San Francisco amalgam of the good, the bad, and the ugly. Many of the city's festivities — the Earth Day celebration, the St. Patrick's Day and

Gay Pride parades — are held there. So are a weekly farmers market and any number of peaceful and not so peaceful protest gatherings. It has also been a lightning rod for the city's homeless for a quarter of a century. At one time, not so long ago, there were permanent encampments that earned it a deserved reputation as a seedy, smelly, high-crime eyesore. The encampments are gone now, but homeless individuals still inhabit the area and the smell of human waste still lingers.

But it's no longer a dangerous place, at least not during the daylight hours. On this bright sunny day, in addition to scattered homeless and panhandling habitués from the nearby skid-row Tenderloin, we passed City Hall employees eating brown-bag lunches on benches and lawn, people walking their dogs, kids playing, an elderly Chinese man practicing Tai Chi, a young couple tossing a Frisbee back and forth.

We found a bench to sit on. While Grace Dellbrook opened her bag and removed her latte, I got out the photograph of Alice Cahill and held it up so that when she turned her head my way she was looking right at it. I was watching for a reaction, but I didn't get one. Not a hint of recognition.

"Who's that?" she asked.

"Alice Cahill."

Her mouth tightened at the corners. "So that's what she looks like. Somehow I thought . . ."

"Thought what?"

"I don't know. That she'd be different, somehow. She doesn't look like a plagiarist."

"What does a plagiarist look like?"

"I don't know; I just had a different image of her." Grace Dellbrook pried the lid off the container of latte. "She *is* a plagiarist. She stole my book, *What the Bride Found Out.* She had no right to do that. No right."

"No, she didn't."

"You know about it? How?"

"Her husband found printouts of some of your e-mail exchanges in her files."

"I'm surprised she kept them." Grace Dellbrook took a swallow of latte that left her with a cream mustache she didn't bother to wipe off. "I always wanted to be a writer," she said then, half-bitterly, half-wistfully, looking past me into the middle distance. "I wrote three books, but no one would publish them. I scrimped and saved enough to pay for *Bride.* It only sold a few copies, but it was *mine* until that woman stole it. Now it isn't anymore. Not even the money will make up for what she did."

"The money you mentioned on the phone."

"Yes. But I haven't received her check yet." She focused on me again. "She *is* still going to pay me? She'd better."

"How much did you agree on?"

"You don't know? Wasn't a printout of those e-mails in her file?"

"No."

"Two thousand dollars. That's what she offered."

"When was this?"

"More than a week ago. The eighteenth."

"The eighteenth is the day Alice Cahill went missing."

Ms. Dellbrook looked startled. "She's been gone that long? What happened to her?"

"That hasn't been determined yet."

"But . . . her last e-mail was written that morning, answering mine of the night before. She said she'd pay right away."

"What did you say in yours?"

"I told her I'd go public with what she did, make a big stink with her publishers if she didn't make things right. I threatened to sue her, too, not that I'd have been able to do it. I went to two different lawyers and they both told me plagiarism is very hard to prove, particularly with a self-published

144

book like mine. It would've cost me more to sue her for copyright infringement than I could ever hope to get."

"Did you ever try to talk to her in person?"

"No. I don't know where she lives and I don't care."

"Were you at work on the eighteenth, the entire day?"

"I haven't missed a day of work in five years, not one single day —" She broke off, blinking, as if struck by a sudden thought. Then, jerkily, "My God, you don't think *I* had anything to do with her going missing? Is that why you're questioning me?"

"You're not under suspicion."

"I'd better not be. I told you, she promised to pay me two thousand dollars for stealing my book. I'll show you her e-mail if you don't believe me."

"That won't be necessary. I believe you." I got to my feet. "Thanks for your time, Ms. Dellbrook."

She said, "Let me ask you something before you go. Do you think Alice Cahill is dead, that someone may have killed her?"

"I can't give you an answer. I deal in facts, not speculation."

"But she could be dead. I won't be surprised if she is." Headshake. "Two thousand dollars. That's a lot of money and now I may never get it. Nothing ever turns out right for me."

There was nothing to say to that. Nothing more to say to her at all. I left her sitting there, a forlorn, white-mustached figure staring off into space again, the cup of latte in one hand and the uneaten muffin in the other.

11

JAKE RUNYON

"Is there any reason I should stay another day, drive home tomorrow instead?" That was the first thing Patricia Dennison said to him when he met her in the lodge's lobby on Friday morning.

"I don't see any reason you should, no."

"Then you haven't learned anything yet. Or expect to today."

"Investigations take time, Mrs. Dennison," Runyon said, hedging. "When I have something definite to report, you'll hear from me right away."

"I'd prefer daily progress reports in any case."

"You'll have them, then."

"Have you spoken to Philip's friend in Sacramento yet, the man who owns the cabin?"

"Briefly on the phone last night. I'll see him later today."

"He'll know who the woman is, if anyone does."

"Possibly."

"Offer him money if you can't get him to tell you any other way. As much as necessary."

Runyon made a throat sound that could have meant agreement but didn't. Resorting to bribery, even the more or less legitimate variety, in order to get information was not the way he operated; that kind of tactic made him and his employers look bad. Besides which, if an insurance agent who owned two homes was greedy enough to accept a bribe, he might also be dishonest enough to lie. There were better ways of finding out what Lloyd Hansen knew about Philip Dennison's love life, if he knew anything pertinent.

"All right," she said. "I couldn't bear to sit around here all day waiting, so I may as well leave as planned."

It was what she'd intended to do all along; she was dressed for traveling in a skirt, blouse, jacket, the dark blond hair neatly combed, and she was carrying her overnight bag. Like him, she didn't mind being alone, preferred it at a crisis point in her life, but she needed movement, activity — he understood that much about her. When she got home, he thought, she'd find things to do to occupy her time, help her cope. Here at Eagle Lake, in an unfamiliar room in the unfamiliar place where her husband had died, she was at loose ends, a prisoner of her emotions.

He waited while she checked out, then drove her to the A-1 Garage to pick up her husband's Cadillac. Went inside with her while she claimed it, stowed her bag in the trunk for her. Before she got in behind the wheel, she said, "I should be back in the city by one o'clock and home for the rest of the day. I'll expect to hear from you."

"You will. Have a safe drive, Mrs. Dennison."

"Thank you." Then, with more meaning than she may have intended, "I intend be very careful from now on."

Runyon was first to arrive at the Hansen cabin, just before noon. He parked the Ford in front of the lean-to, went to have the look around that he'd been denied yesterday.

He made a slow circuit of the cabin, the thick carpeting of pine needles and meadow grass spongy underfoot. The smells of pine resin and new spring growth were sharp on the warm morning air. Out on the lake, a couple of skiffs were gliding along in opposite directions, their occupants taking advantage of the sunny weather. The faint pulsing of outboard motors and the chatter of birds were the only sounds.

The cabin had five windows altogether, four of them with the inside shutters closed. Runyon stopped at the unshuttered side window that had been broken and repaired by Joe Meeker. When he stepped up close and made a frame with his hands against the glass, he could see the interior clearly. He stood peering in for several seconds, then shifted position on the sloping ground, first left, then right, then up on his toes. He was still looking, the muscles along his jaw-line rippling, when he heard the vehicle rumble in off the road.

Dark blue four-door Honda, not more than four years old. The thirty something who got out of it and walked toward him had dark red hair, a pudgy body encased in slacks and a tan safari jacket, and a round, florid face with features that, up close, seemed disproportionately small. The smile he wore was tentative, on the wary side, as if he'd been having second thoughts about the advisability of this meeting. Runyon's size, chiseled features, and sober expression did nothing to put him at ease.

"Mr. Runyon? Lloyd Hansen."

They shook hands. Hansen's clasp was loose, the release quick, as though he were leery of having his fingers crushed.

Runyon said, "I appreciate this, Mr. Hansen."

"Well, under the circumstances . . ." Hansen let the rest of what he'd been about to say trail off. He moved over to peer at the new pane of glass puttied into the window frame. "Looks like Joe Meeker did a good job."

"Has he done other repair work for you?"

"Some."

"Know him well?"

"I wouldn't say that, no. Not very talkative, keeps to himself, but he's reliable enough."

"Have you met his wife?"

"Couple of times, over at the café." Hansen's mouth stretch stopped just short of being a smirk. "Quite a good-looking woman."

"Very friendly, too, I understand."

"So I've been told. I wouldn't know from personal experience."

"Philip Dennison's type?"

The grin faded. "I have no idea."

"He never mentioned her to you?"

"No."

"What was his type?"

151

"His wife, I suppose. I never met her, but Phil carried a picture in his wallet. . . ." Hansen let the sentence trail off and made a throat-clearing noise. "Look, let's go inside. I need to see what's what in there."

Runyon had been about to suggest the same thing. He nodded, followed Hansen up onto the porch and then inside after he unlocked the door. Hansen left the door open, saying, "Musty in here, needs airing out."

He switched on the lights, stood looking around and shaking his head, then went to the fireplace and bent to stare at the hearthstones. "Christ," he said. "There's a big bloodstain where Phil cracked his head. How am I going to get it out? Bleach?"

Runyon didn't answer. He'd turned to examine the inside of the door. There was a small hole, almost a gouge, a few inches above the door handle and lock. He took a closer look, ran his finger over it. Fairly deep. Fresh.

He moved over to lift the two-by-four wooden bar. The edges had nicks and scratches from use, none of them recent. But near one end he found a vertical scrape some five inches long and shallow. That, too, appeared to be newly made.

Behind him Hansen said, "What're you

doing there?"

"Same as you. Looking around."

"The place is a mess. Bloodstains. Broken glass. God knows what else." He went to the hallway, down it to the partially open door to the bedroom.

Runyon walked around, bent at the waist and peering at the floor. There was nothing to see along the walls on either side of the door. He moved over to the near end of the couch. When he bent low to peer underneath, something on the floor next to the nearest leg caught his eye — something small and metallic.

In the bedroom Hansen was making rustling, flapping noises. Then he let out a surprised bleat, followed it with an exasperated, "Oh, for God's sake."

On one knee, Runyon fished out the shiny object and picked it up with thumb and forefinger. Nail. Two inches long, slightly bent, free of dust. He was still looking at it when Hansen came out of the bedroom.

"What've you got there?"

"The answer, maybe."

"Answer? Answer to what?"

"Never mind. It's a nail." He held it up for Hansen to see, then dropped it into his shirt pocket.

"Bedroom and bathroom are a mess, too,"

Hansen said. He sounded disgusted, annoyed; his florid face was even redder now. "Dirty sheets, dirty towels. Phil didn't even bother to get rid of —"

"Get rid of what?"

Head wag. "This cabin will never be the same again. Ruined for me, I'll have to put it up for sale. The real estate market's lousy now, but I don't think I can stand to spend any more vacation time here."

"What didn't Dennison get rid of, Mr. Hansen?"

"It doesn't matter."

"It might."

". . . Oh, hell, go into the bedroom and look for yourself. On the floor in front of the bed."

Runyon went in there and looked. The rustling and flapping sounds had been Hansen yanking at a down comforter and top sheet on the double bed; they were pulled half off on one side. At first glance, what lay on the bare wood at the foot of the bed resembled the wrinkled shed skin of a snake. A condom was what it was, one of the kind called a French Tickler. Unwrapped and rolled out full length.

"Damn thing was caught up in the sheet." Hansen had come into the doorway behind him. "Why would Phil unroll it if he didn't use it?"

Runyon didn't reply.

"Hole in it, maybe," Hansen said, answering his own question.

They went back into the front room. Hansen leaned against the side of the highback couch, the expression on his chubby red face morose. "Well?" he said. "Are you satisfied?"

"Not yet."

"What more do you need? Phil had a woman here. That's what you wanted to know, isn't it?"

"But it wasn't the woman he planned to meet."

"How do you know that?"

"She didn't show. Canceled out at the last minute."

"Why would she do that? I thought . . ."

"What did you think?"

Another headshake. "So Phil went out and picked up some bimbo instead. So what?"

Runyon said again, "What did you think? That the woman he was supposed to meet was more than just a casual lay? That they were involved in a relationship?"

"I don't want to talk about that."

"I do. The other times your friend Dennison borrowed this cabin — was it to meet the same woman each time?"

". . . I don't know."

"You do know. *Was* it the same woman?"

Hansen did some struggling with himself. At length he said, "Well, shit. Phil's dead; he as much as killed himself here and ruined the cabin for me; why should I bother to cover for him now. Yes, it was the same woman."

"Her name?"

"Lucia something. I don't know her last name."

"Sure about that?"

"I don't think Phil ever mentioned it."

"Where does she live?"

"San Francisco. Owns or runs some kind of boutique downtown. He went in there one day to buy something; that's how he met her."

"Where downtown?"

"He didn't say and I didn't ask."

"How long had the affair been going on?"

"I don't know," Hansen said, "a long time. Off and on. Best lay he ever had, he said, he couldn't get enough of her. I could believe it, the way she looked."

"He show you a picture of her or did you meet her?"

"Met her, once. She was with him the second time he came to my office for the cabin key. Silky black hair, olive skin, great legs. Seemed nice, too, kind of shy." Hansen nibbled at his heavy underlip. "I was a little jealous, you want to know the truth. I don't cheat on my wife, but if I had the chance with a woman like Lucia, I'd be real tempted."

Runyon said, "You said it was an off-and-on affair. Meaning?"

"Well . . . he was stringing her along — you know, the old bit about promising to divorce his wife and marry her — and now and then she'd balk and break it off. But then old Silver Tongue would talk her into coming back. I felt sorry for her. His wife, too."

"Then why did you keep on aiding and abetting him?"

Hansen spread his hands, palms up — a self-defensive gesture. "He was an old friend, that's why. We were roommates for three years at Sac State; we had a lot of good times together. Hell, it was none of my business if he had a woman on the side or how he treated her. That's what I kept telling myself, anyway."

Runyon had had enough of Lloyd Hansen. He'd found out as much as he needed to know about Philip Dennison's love life, and considerably more besides. Other things to do now, a different kind of important business to attend to.

Before he left he said, "Don't be surprised if you see me again today. I expect to be back fairly soon, with company."

"Company? Who?"

"You'll find out when the time comes."

12

JAKE RUNYON

On his way back to the village he put in a call to Tamara at the agency. Got through all right; the cell phone service today was reasonably clear. She'd run the checks on the numbers from Philip Dennison's address book he'd e-mailed her, but none belonged to either a downtown S.F. boutique or a woman named Lucia, or to anyone with a name that resembled *Lucia*. Tamara said she'd see if she could make a connection, get back to him later.

She'd also done the background check on Patricia Dennison and e-mailed him the data. He asked if there were any facts of particular interest that pertained to her relationship with her husband; Tamara said she didn't think so. The specifics, then, could wait until later.

He went straight to the sheriff's substation. Rittenhouse was on duty today, but out with another deputy investigating a road accident. The dispatcher didn't know when he was likely to return.

So then Runyon drove to Eagle Lake Clinic, asked to speak with Dr. Wolfe. Better luck there; Wolfe was present and available for a brief consultation. He came out to meet Runyon at the admittance desk in the lobby — a middle-aged, heavyset man with bulldog jowls and a gruff manner. The gruffness was offset by mild blue eyes and an air of professionalism.

"My name is Runyon, Doctor. I was here yesterday with Deputy Rittenhouse and Mrs. Dennison."

"Yes, I remember. What can I do for you?"

"Answer a few questions about Philip Dennison. I understand he was intoxicated when he died."

"No question about that," Wolfe said. "The body still reeked of alcohol when it was brought in."

"What can you tell me about the wound that killed him?"

"The basilar part of the occipital bone was crushed."

"That's at the back of the skull."

"Yes."

"Were there any other wounds or marks on the head or body?"

160

"Why do you ask that?"

"I assure you, it's not idle curiosity."

"The man died in a drunken fall inside a locked cabin. His death was a simple, if tragic, accident."

"I'd still like to know about other wounds or marks."

Wolfe looked as though his competency was being called into question. He said through pursed lips, "There was a contusion on the left cheekbone."

"What sort of contusion? Large, deep?"

"Neither. Are you suggesting the man's death was *not* accidental?"

"I'm not suggesting anything. Just looking for information."

"In my opinion," Wolfe said stiffly, "the contusion occurred postmortem, a result of the body, after the fatal blow had been struck, rebounding sideways so that the cheek was lacerated and the malar bone slightly damaged by the hearthstones. Does that answer your question?"

It did, but not in the way Dr. Wolfe thought.

Rittenhouse still hadn't returned to the substation. But he'd radioed in, the dispatcher said, and expected to be back within the half hour. Runyon took a seat in the visitors' area, spent a little time mentally clarifying what he'd learned and what he suspected, and then utilized the knack he'd developed of shutting his mind down during periods of waiting. He sat so still he might have been asleep with his eyes open. The dispatcher apparently thought so; from the way she kept glancing over at him, she'd never seen anyone sit unmoving for such a long time while still awake and alert.

He was on his feet as soon as the door opened and Rittenhouse came in. The chief deputy gave him a look that wasn't quite neutral. Neither was Rittenhouse's voice when he said, "Waiting for me, Mr. Runyon?"

"Yes. Some things I need to discuss with you."

"I thought we covered everything yesterday."

"Not everything. Not at all."

"I don't know what else I can tell you."

"It's what I can tell you this time. Can we talk privately?"

"As long as it doesn't take too long. I've got an accident report to make out."

"What I have to say won't take too long. What happens after that probably will."

Rittenhouse said, frowning, "That's a cryptic statement if I ever heard one. All right, we'll talk in my office."

His office was small and unadorned except for a county seal on one wall that duplicated the one in the outer room, and a framed certificate from the California Peace Officers Association. He took off his hat, put it on an old-fashioned file cabinet, then sat behind a gray metal desk; Runyon pulled a straight-backed chair up in front of it.

"What is it you have to tell me, Mr. Runyon?"

"A request first. I assume photographs were taken in the cabin before Philip Dennison's body was removed."

"Standard procedure, even in cases of accidental death."

"I'd like to see them."

"Why?"

"To make sure I'm on the right track."

"The right track. Meaning what?"

"Can I see the photos? Then I'll explain."

The deputy ran a finger over the patch of eczema on his pink scalp, shrugged, and booted up the computer on a stand alongside his desk. He pulled up the Dennison file, located the photographs. Then he got to his feet and moved away from the desk, saying, "Go ahead and look."

Runyon went around to sit in Rittenhouse's chair. The first photograph showed him what he'd expected to see, and some-

163

thing more. There were four others, taken from different angles; these confirmed his suspicion beyond any doubt. He stood, went back around to the other chair.

"Well?" Rittenhouse said.

"What I wanted to check on was the location and position of the body. Not quite directly in front of the fireplace — back a little ways, smashed head toward the door."

"I could have told you that."

"If he'd slipped on the rug and fallen, drunk or sober, the body wouldn't have been lying as it was."

"You can see the rug bunched up under his feet —"

"Look at his arms, Deputy. When a man slips and falls, his instinctive reaction is to throw his arms out in front him to break the fall. Dennison's should have been stretched out in front of him, but they're not; they're drawn back against his sides."

Rittenhouse swiveled around to the computer, clicked through the photos. "You're right. That never even occurred to me."

"No reason it should have, under the circumstances."

"So how do you explain it?"

"A few questions first," Runyon said. "Were you the one who broke the window so you could get inside the cabin?"

"No. Joe Meeker did that with a hammer from his tool belt."

"Did you take a good look through the glass before he did?"

". . . No. There was sunlight on the glass by then and you couldn't see inside clearly. No reason not to take Meeker at his word."

"What time was that?"

"Nine o'clock or so."

"Once you were inside, was any of the furniture moved? The couch?"

"No. There wasn't any reason to move anything. What difference does any of this make anyway? The place was locked up tight, just as Meeker told us — Fred Johnson, the other deputy, and I checked first to make sure. The only way to get in was to break the window."

"The only unshuttered window. The one Meeker said he spotted the body through."

"That's right. So?"

"So you can't see the front part of the fireplace looking through that window from outside," Runyon said. "The high-backed couch, which you say wasn't moved, blocks it from any angle. I know because I tried myself around noon, when there was no sunlight on the glass. You'd have to stand on a ladder and look down through the top part of the glass, and even then you might not have a clear view."

Rittenhouse sat still for several seconds. "You're saying Meeker lied. Then how did he know Dennison was dead inside?"

"He knew because he killed him."

"*Killed* him?" The deputy was incredulous. "Joe Meeker? Why, for God's sake?"

"His wife was the woman Dennison was sleeping with — that's pretty obvious. I think Meeker came home earlier than expected from his hunting trip, suspected or found out somehow, and beat the truth out of her — that bruise on her cheek. He went to the cabin in a jealous rage to confront Dennison. Not necessarily to kill him, but that's how it ended up."

"You're forgetting that the cabin was closed up."

"No, I'm not. The front door lock wasn't secure, was it? The dead bolt, I mean."

". . . No. But the door was barred, I told you that."

"Meeker rigged it to support an accident verdict. His big mistake was coming to fetch you the next morning. He might've gotten away with it if he hadn't. You'll have to ask him why."

"*How* could he have rigged it? He's no genius."

"Doesn't take a genius to do what he did.

Just a quick-thinking handyman and maybe ten minutes of effort, start to finish."

"Well, what did he do? Dennison could have let him in, sure, but I don't see any way Meeker could've gotten back out again with that crossbar in place, the back door and all the windows locked tight."

"Come out to the cabin with me," Runyon said, "and I'll show you how he did it."

The eczema on Rittenhouse's scalp got a fingernail workout while he thought it over. At length he said darkly, "Are you sure you're right about this, Runyon? Absolutely sure?"

"Yes."

"All right, then I've got a better idea. We'll find Joe Meeker first and the three of us will go to the cabin. You can show me how he did it with him standing right there."

13

The Prime Medical Group was located in a large complex on Ygnacio Valley Road not far from the John Muir Medical Center. It shared space with a number of other physicians' practices, most of which seemed to offer specialty medical services. The waiting room was large, pristine, and about a quarter full when I walked in a few minutes ahead of my three o'clock appointment with Dr. Paul Nesbitt.

Like most people, I have an aversion to hospitals and doctors' offices. Too many visits to both over the course of my life, all too often the result of one crisis or another. Invariably, just walking into a place like this scrapes my nerves and raises my blood pressure, so I stay out of them as much as possible. Which is why I keep putting off annual physicals. It had been eighteen months since my last checkup and Kerry had been nagging at me to bite the bullet and get it done. I'd promised her I would, and I don't break my promises, but I still hadn't made the damn appointment. All right, then, I told myself as I sat twitching in the Prime Group's waiting area, if you don't do it soon the next time Kerry brings it up she'll do it for you and how will that make you feel? Like a promise breaker after all. Like a big baby.

Fortunately, Dr. Nesbitt didn't keep me hanging long. A plump nurse or nurse practitioner — you couldn't tell which these days, uniforms being a thing of the past and casual dress the new norm — came out to fetch me. She led me along a couple of interior hallways, past cubicles containing blood pressure machines and scales and the like, past open and closed consulting room doors, and finally into a medium-sized private office where she shut me in with Dr. Paul Nesbitt.

He stood waiting in front of a desk covered with papers, medical journals, X-ray photographs, and one of those handheld computers doctors and nurses use these days. He gave me a stone-faced once-over, shook my hand in a perfunctory manner as if I might be a germ carrier, and invited me to sit down. Maybe it was his manner or where we were, but he didn't need a stethoscope around his neck or a white smock or green scrubs to look exactly like what he was. In fact, he could have played the lead role on one of those TV doctor shows, perfectly cast according to Hollywood standards. Full head of wavy brown hair dusted with gray at the temples. Kirk Douglas cleft in his chin. Symmetrical features and large brown eyes that radiated intelligence and cool competence.

I didn't like him. He made me feel old, fat, semi-ugly, and even more of a cowardly delinquent for putting off my annual physical. Irrational reaction, but even though I knew it was first-impression nonsense, I could not seem to work through it. The words sounded pinched when I said, "Thank you for seeing me, Doctor. I wasn't sure you'd agree to an interview."

"No? Because of the conversation you had with my wife, I suppose."

"She was somewhat hostile, yes."

"Naturally she was. She doesn't like this sort of thing any more than I do."

"What sort of thing?"

Abruptly, "Just what is it you expect to accomplish?"

"Excuse me?"

"The police haven't been able to determine what happened to Alice Cahill. What

170

makes you and her husband think you can? Assuming, of course, that he isn't responsible?"

Nesbitt's voice was about as warm as a scoop of Italian ice. He did not like me any more than I liked him. Well, that was dandy. The sense of mutual antipathy banished my feeling of insecurity, made dealing with him a little easier. Supercilious, antagonistic types raise my hackles, prod me into adopting a more aggressive attitude than I usually take with strangers.

I said, "I take it you don't believe the man is entitled to an advocate."

"I didn't say that."

"You didn't have to. Innocent until proven guilty, Doctor."

"I suppose that means you believe his hands are clean?"

"I just stated my position. When I agree to represent a client, my job is similar to that of an attorney. Do whatever I can for him."

"That doesn't answer my question," Nesbitt said. "Is it your belief that he's innocent?"

"Is it yours that he's guilty?"

"I don't see how anyone else could be."

"What do you suppose happened? He killed her in a drunken rage?"

"Hardly that. Jim Cahill is not given to drunken rages."

"Your wife told me he drinks to excess, that he and his wife had violent quarrels when he was drunk."

The good doctor seemed not to know how to respond to that. At length he said stiffly, "Kendra exaggerates," and let it go at that.

"When did you last see Mrs. Cahill?"

"What difference does it make when I saw her last?"

"You're her physician. Did she do or say anything that might help explain what happened to her?"

"No, she did not."

"And when was that last visit?"

"A few days before she disappeared." He adjusted the knot in his silk tie, even though it didn't need adjusting. "Just what do you hope to accomplish with all this poking around in private lives?"

"Such as yours, you mean?"

His lips compressed so tightly his mouth resembled a scalpel slash. When he spoke again, it was with an obvious effort to maintain his composure. "You won't find out what happened to Alice that way."

"You sound very sure of that."

"I *am* sure. You haven't learned anything yet that might exonerate him, have you?"

"Oh, I've made a little headway."

"What sort of headway?"

"I'm not at liberty to say. You have doctor-patient confidentiality; I have detective-client confidentiality."

He waited a few seconds before he said, "If you persist in trying to dig up dirt in a misguided effort to assist your client, you'll regret it."

"Dirt, Doctor?"

". . . A poor choice of words. But you understand my point, I trust."

I understood it, all right — the real reason Nesbitt had been willing to talk to me. He didn't seem to care much, if he cared at all, what had happened to his friend and patient Alice Cahill. What he cared about was himself, protecting his privacy. Why? What was it he was afraid I might find out?

"It's been my experience," I said, "that if a person has nothing to hide, an investigation can't do him or her any harm."

"Are you insinuating I have something to hide?"

"Do you?"

"Certainly not. I have a strong dislike of unwarranted prying, that's all. I meant what I said; I won't tolerate it."

"And I won't tolerate unwarranted threats. I intend to continue doing the job I was hired to do, Doctor, whether you and your wife like it or not."

Nesbitt put his hands flat on the desktop, levered himself to his feet. "I'll thank you to leave now. I have patients to see."

"People whose welfare is as important to you as your own?" I could not resist the jibe. He brought out the worst in me.

The scalpel-slash mouth again. And an eye glare that cut into me like a laser. He had nothing more to say. Neither did I; I stood as quickly as he had and went, feeling a whole lot better about myself than I had coming in.

Streeter Manufacturing was housed in a large, modern building in a newish industrial park on the outskirts of Concord. What they manufactured, according to a sign in front, was compact refrigerators, wine coolers, and icemakers. Judging from the size of the place and the expensively furnished reception area, the firm was a model of commercial success.

I told the young receptionist that I had an appointment with James Cahill. One minute after she notified him I was there, out he came looking tired and harried and conducted me down an interior hallway and into a good-sized office with wall-to-wall carpeting, blond wood furnishings, and a couple of windows overlooking what had once been an expanse of lawn and was now just another dead brown victim of the drought.

As soon as he shut the door he said with a kind of pathetic eagerness that was at once hopeful and hopeless, "Have you found out anything yet?"

I would have to tell him that his wife was in fact a plagiarist and had offered Grace Dellbrook two thousand dollars to keep it covered up, but this was neither the time nor the place. He had plenty on his mind already, and I was about to give him more — issues that did have to be dealt with immediately.

"Nothing specific," I said. "I'm still gathering information. I have some questions that require answers, as I told you when we spoke earlier."

"Anything you want to know. Can I get you something first? Coffee, a soda?"

"Nothing, thanks." We sat down. "Let's start with the insurance," I said.

Blank look. "Insurance?"

"The hundred-thousand-dollar joint life policy you and your wife have. You didn't tell me about it. Why not?"

"I forgot it. Honest to God, it never even

entered my mind." Now he looked cha-grined, apologetic. "How did you find out about it?"

"Kendra Nesbitt. She thinks it's one of the reasons you did away with your wife."

"That's crazy. Jesus. Alice isn't dead; she's just missing." He couldn't sit still. Up on his feet, moving back and forth behind his chrome-and-glass desk. "Even if I wanted to collect on it, and I don't, I couldn't if she isn't found. Not for, what is it, seven years?"

"That's right, seven years."

"I'd have to be crazy myself to wait that long for money. I don't care about money, I care about Alice. Jesus."

The earnest pleading in his voice wasn't faked; his eyes, his body language, would have given him away if it had been. I'd already dismissed the insurance angle, but it had needed to be mentioned, Cahill's response noted, in order to be written off completely.

"Do you drink to excess, Mr. Cahill?"

"What? No. No. What gave you that idea?"

"Never fought with your wife in a drunken rage?"

"No, of course not. We hardly ever fought at all, except when she was in one of her dark moods, and then all I ever did was try to calm her down. . . ."

Cahill sat down again, dry-washed his face with one hand. "Who told you all those lies? Kendra?"

"Yes."

"She must really hate me to make up crap like that."

"You give her cause to hate you?"

"No. We never got along very well, I think I told you that yesterday, but all we ever did was exchange a few sharp words when she tried to interfere."

"Interfere in your relationship with your wife?"

"She never thought I was good enough, strong enough, for Alice. Always trying to talk her into divorcing me, not that it did her any good. Alice would never leave me voluntarily. She loves me, depends on me."

"So she didn't listen to her sister."

"No, and it drove Kendra crazy. They argued all the time."

"She says there was no friction, no sibling rivalry, between them."

"That's another lie. There was. Ask Fran Woodward, she'll confirm it."

"I already have," I said. "And she did. A love-hate sibling relationship, in her opinion."

"I don't know that I'd go that far, but . . . they went at it pretty heavily sometimes.

Verbally, I mean."

"Did you ever threaten to harm your wife?"

"My God, no."

"Or her sister?"

"No," Cahill said. "All I ever did was tell Kendra to butt out of our affairs. Not so politely a couple of times, but never in a threatening way."

"What about Dr. Nesbitt? Have any problems with him?"

"No. He didn't pester Alice the way Kendra did."

"Does he agree with her, you think? That your wife would be better off divorcing you?"

"He never said anything if he does. Not to me."

"So then you get along with him."

"I suppose so."

"Suppose so?"

"Well, we don't interact much," Cahill said. "Paul . . . he's not the sort of man you can know well, at least that I've been able to know well. Have you talked to him yet?"

"Before I came here."

"Then maybe you understand what I mean."

"Kind of a cold fish. Full of himself."

Cahill nodded. "That pretty much sums

him up. But he's not a bad guy, really. And he's a good doctor. Very attentive to Alice, helped her get through some of her worst periods."

"How would you categorize his marriage?"

"It's pretty solid, I guess. I mean, he and Kendra have been married a long time and they seem to get along all right. She can be bossy as hell, but he just ignores her when she's like that."

"There's one other thing she told me," I said. "That you're having an affair with one of your co-workers, Megan Sprague."

Cahill jerked as if he'd been goosed. His collar was suddenly tight; he tugged at it with a forefinger just above the knot in his tie. He did not quite flush, but little streaks of red showed on his neck.

"Well, Mr. Cahill?"

"How . . . how would Kendra know a thing like that?"

"She wouldn't say. Is it true?"

"No. Not —" He tugged at his collar again. "Not exactly."

"That's not an answer. Either it's true or it isn't."

"Megan and I, we're just friends. I can talk to her; she's been very supportive. . . ."

"So you're not sleeping with her. Even

though by your own admission it's been six months since you had relations with your wife."

The red streaks grew a little darker. "All right. Once. That's all, I swear to God, one night about four months ago. We . . . after that we decided it'd been a mistake and we're better off keeping our friendship platonic. I never cheated on Alice before that one time; I'm not that kind of husband. You have to believe that."

"If it weren't for your wife, would you and Ms. Sprague remain just friends?"

". . . I don't know what you mean."

"Sure you do. How much of a bond is there between you? If you weren't married any longer, if you were a widower, would the two of you get together on a permanent basis?"

"I . . . I can't answer that. I care for Megan, but I don't love her."

"Could you love her if circumstances permitted?"

"I suppose so. We're compatible, we . . . oh, Christ."

"How does she feel? Would she be open to a permanent relationship?"

"I don't know. She's never said anything."

"Never mentioned it, never indicated how deep her feelings are for you?"

"No. We're just friends; I told you that
—"

"You also told me you slept with her once.
How was it? Good for both of you?"

Cahill shoved his chair back so abruptly
the headrest cracked against the wall behind
him, climbed onto his feet again. There was
plenty of color in his face now; it was the
first time I'd seen him show strong emotion. I was not proud of the way I'd goaded
him, but I wanted to see how he'd react.
Angrily, but not violently. His eyes didn't
bulge; his fists didn't clench. He just stood
there staring at me like an animal that had
just been kicked.

"That was a lousy thing to say," he said in
a choked voice.

"I know it. And I apologize. But if I'm going to keep on working for you, I have to
have the truth, the whole truth, and nothing
but. No lies, nothing withheld."

The anger went out of him, loosening the
muscles in his face and body; he sank down
into the chair again. "I haven't lied to you,"
he said, "and there's nothing else I haven't
told you."

"All right. Does Ms. Sprague know you
hired me?"

"Yes. I told her last night." He added, "On

the phone," so I wouldn't get the wrong idea.

"Is she here now?"

". . . Yes?" Making a question out of the word.

"Would you mind introducing me to her?"

That stiffened his spine again. "Why? You don't intend to ask her about our relationship —"

"No, I won't do that."

"Then why do you want to —" A sudden thought came to him; you could see it in the widening of his eyes. "My God, you don't think *she* had anything to do with Alice's disappearance? That's insane! Megan is kind, gentle . . . she's incapable of hurting anyone for any reason."

Just friends except for one lapse? Well, maybe. But the way he'd rushed to her defense, the words he'd used to describe her, indicated that his feelings for her might be stronger than he was willing to admit, to me or to himself.

"I don't think anything," I said. "Just doing my job the best way I know how. Do you object to my meeting her?"

He blew out a breath before he said, "No, of course not." He picked up the phone on his desk, tapped out an extension number. "Megan? Would you come to my office for a minute?"

It did not take her long to get there. Light rap on the door, and she came in smiling, stopped when she saw me get up off my chair. She was about Cahill's age, copper-brown hair cut short and swept back on both sides, wide-set hazel eyes, slender, the hem of her green skirt cut high enough to show off shapely legs. She had the kind of face that you hear described as having character, a polite way of saying that the more you look at a woman who seems plain at first, the more attractive you realize she is. When she moved again, it was with her head cocked slightly to one side in a quizzical sort of way.

Cahill introduced us. She didn't need to say she was glad to meet me; the eyes, the smile, the firm handshake, said it for her.

"Have you found out something? Is that why you're here?"

"Not yet, no."

"Do you think there's any chance you will?"

"Hard to say. I'm doing my best."

"I'm sure you are. Mr. Cahill is at his wit's end, with all the false accusations and innuendo. He had absolutely nothing to do with his wife's disappearance."

Defending him openly, with a sideways

glance at him as she spoke. She cared about him, all right. Just how much was open to question, but if I'd had to make an immediate guess I would have said that her feelings ran deeper than a simple friend with one-time benefit. Over the years I've learned to trust my first impressions, up to a point; the one I had of her was favorable. She struck me as a woman of unswerving loyalty, the kind of person you'd want in your corner in a crisis. Of course, loyalty can be carried to extremes if it's mixed with a passionate and mostly unrequited love. I did not know enough about Megan Sprague to make any definite judgment about her.

As for Cahill, I was getting to know him well enough to judge that he was driven by his emotions and that they made him both deferential and unpredictable. Three minutes ago he'd been worried that I would say something to Ms. Sprague about their relationship. Now, impulsively, he said to her, "My damn sister-in-law told him she thinks we're having an affair, that that's one of the reasons I did something to Alice."

She didn't flinch. Didn't lose her composure in any way. She said to me in the same even voice, "It's not true. Mrs. Nesbitt made it up. She has it in for Jim, God knows why."

"We're just friends," Cahill said. "I told him that."

"Yes. Just friends."

I asked, "How do you suppose Mrs. Nesbitt came to that conclusion?"

"I have no idea. Jim?"

"She didn't get it from Alice. I never said a word to Alice about you." The additional words *and me* were in his open mouth, but he didn't allow them to come out.

"You don't believe it, do you?" Megan Sprague asked me. "That Jim would harm his wife because of me?"

"No," I said, "I don't."

"Good. It's pure nonsense. Whatever happened to poor Mrs. Cahill, it had nothing to do with Jim."

If she'd added, *Or with me,* I might have marked her down a notch in my estimation. But she didn't. She just stood there, straight and staunch, no longer smiling — a rock. The kind of rock a man like Cahill needed, the kind of rock his wife hadn't been.

14

JAKE RUNYON

Locating Joe Meeker proved to be easy. Rittenhouse drove first to Meeker's cabin, and the handyman's Silverado pickup was parked there in plain sight from the road. They found him inside his workshop stripping varnish from an old walnut hutch.

As soon as he saw them, he was on his guard. You could see his thin, bony face close up, the smoke-colored eyes darken and then narrow. He gave Runyon a cursory glance, then held his gaze on the chief deputy.

"What's up, Charlie?" he asked.

"We need you to come over to the Hansen cabin with us."

"What, right now? What for?"

"We'll talk about that when we get there."

"Can't it wait? I'm pretty busy —"

"No, it can't wait. Now."

"How come you brought this guy here

186

with you?" Meeker said, still keeping his eyes off Runyon. "What's he got to do with whatever's going on?"

"At the cabin," Rittenhouse said. "You're not going to give me any trouble, are you, Joe?"

"Trouble? Me? Hell, no. I'm just confused, that's all."

"Better take off your tool belt before we go."

"Oh, sure." Meeker slid the screwdriver he'd been using into a belt slot, unbuckled the belt, and laid it on the workbench. His hands were steady enough doing that and then wiping them on an already grease-stained rag. He had nerve, Runyon thought, not that that was any surprise given his actions on Tuesday night. "You want me to follow you over there?"

"No. We'll go in my cruiser."

They trooped outside, Meeker with his skinny shoulders squared. Rittenhouse unlocked the cruiser's rear door for him — prisoner's seating, behind the thick wire mesh screen that divided the interior in half. But he didn't say anything, didn't hesitate, just shrugged and got in.

Nobody said anything on the short drive to the Hansen cabin. Runyon half-turned on the front seat to watch Meeker through the mesh, a psychological ploy he'd learned in his time on the Seattle PD. But it didn't rattle the little handyman. He kept his head turned away, looking or pretending to look out through the side window.

Lloyd Hansen's Honda was parked in the same place as before. Runyon had told the deputy about his earlier meeting with the cabin's owner, that Hansen was liable to still be here when they arrived. Rittenhouse said it wouldn't be a problem.

Meeker sat forward as they turned onto the property. "Whose car is that: Mr. Hansen's? We come here to see him?"

"No," Rittenhouse said. He braked alongside the Honda. "I'll go talk to Hansen. You two wait here."

"Listen," Meeker said as the deputy moved away toward the cabin. "What's this all about, huh?"

Runyon didn't answer.

"You trying to get me in trouble with the law for some reason? I never done nothing."

No response to that, either. Let him sweat in silence.

Rittenhouse was in the cabin less than five minutes. When he came out, Lloyd Hansen was with him. They split up as they neared the parked vehicles, Hansen going to his car, the deputy to the passenger side of the cruiser. He stood there while Hansen started the Honda, swung it around and up onto the road. Once it was out of sight, Rittenhouse motioned to Runyon and Meeker to get out and join him.

"You tell Mr. Hansen to leave?" Meeker asked the deputy. "Where's he going?"

"Into the village to do some shopping. We'll be gone by the time he gets back."

"We going into the cabin or what?"

"Not just yet."

Rittenhouse led the way to the side window. Meeker said then, "I put in a new pane of glass yesterday. Didn't ask your permission, but I figured it'd be okay to go ahead."

The deputy said nothing. He leaned up close to the window, made a frame of his hands, peered inside. As Runyon had done earlier, he moved first one way, then the other, then stretched up on his toes.

When he turned he said to Meeker, "I can't see the front of the fireplace, Joe."

"Huh?"

"You heard me. I can't see it from the low angle here and I'm four inches taller than you. The high back of the couch is in the way."

Meeker was getting it now; his expression remained impassive, but the cords in his neck tightened visibly. "What're you saying?

That I didn't see the dead guy like I told you?"

"You couldn't have unless you stood on a ladder," Rittenhouse said, "and probably not even then. You lied to Fred and me."

"No, you're wrong. I didn't see *all* of him lying there, just his head and one of his arms stretched out past the side of the couch —"

"That's impossible. His arms weren't stretched out; they were pulled back against his sides."

". . . I tell you, I saw him. How'd I know he was in there, dead, otherwise?"

Runyon spoke for the first time. "You knew because you were inside with him when he died."

Meeker turned on him. "Like hell! I was never in that cabin!" But the angry denial didn't come off. Forced, phony, edged with desperation. "Who're you to accuse me of killing somebody?"

"He didn't accuse you of murder," Rittenhouse said. "He just said you were inside when Dennison died."

"How could I of been? For Chrissake, the place was locked up tighter'n a drum; you know that, you and Fred checked all the doors and windows —"

Runyon said, "I know how you did it."

"Did it? Did what?"

"Rigged the front door."

Meeker's face underwent a slow color change, chameleon-like, from angry red to ashy gray. "Rigged it? You're crazy. I couldn't have, nobody could."

"A handyman your size could."

"Barred, it was *barred* on the inside." Sputtering now, losing his cool. "Charlie, you know it was with that two-by-four —"

"All right, Runyon," Rittenhouse said. "Suppose we go in and you show us how he did it."

They went around to the front porch, Meeker protesting and casting eye darts at Runyon, and inside. All the living room window shutters were folded back now, two windows opened to rid the interior of the musty odor. Hansen had done some cleanup work as well; there were three filled garbage bags on the plank floor, cleaning solvent and rags on the hearth.

With the door closed again, Runyon took the bent nail from the pocket of his shirt, held it up in front of Meeker. "Recognize this?"

". . . A nail, so what?"

"I found it this morning partway under the couch, where it bounced when it pulled loose and fell."

Rittenhouse said, "Pulled loose and fell from where?"

Runyon showed him the nail hole on the door near its edge, above the knob and lock and a couple of inches higher than where the iron bracket on that side was mounted. "That's where Meeker hammered it in, not too deep, quarter of an inch or so. Then he set one end of the crossbar into the bracket on the hinged side, rested the other end on the nail. Eyeball it and you'll see the door can still be opened inward a few inches with the bar set in that diagonal position. Just far enough for a man as thin as Meeker to squeeze through."

"Bullshit!" the handyman cried.

Runyon lifted the redwood two-by-four, pointed out the vertical gouge. "This was made by the bracket digging into it during the squeeze. Once he was outside, all he had to do was yank the door closed with enough force to dislodge the nail — once or twice would have done it. That's how the nail got bent. When it came loose and fell, the upper end of the bar dropped into the bracket and completed the seal. Simple as that."

Rittenhouse said, "Well, I'll be damned."

Meeker pawed desperately at the deputy's sleeve. "Why would I do something like that, for Chrissake? *Why?*"

"To hide the fact you killed Philip Dennison."

"No, I never did, I had no reason —"

"You had a reason, or thought you did. He was sleeping with Verna while you were off on your hunting trip."

"Oh, Jesus. . . ."

"You came back early and found out. Was she here when you had it out with Dennison? Does she know you killed him?"

Runyon had seen felons crumble any number of times, and it always happened more or less the same way once they'd been caught out. First there was the panicked inclination to run. Then, when they realized they had no chance of getting away, no place to go if they did, the tension and the bluster seeped out of them like water out of a punctured sack; their bodies went limp as if collapsing in on themselves, their eyes darkened and dulled with defeat, resignation, shimmers of fear. He watched it happen to Joe Meeker, watched the handyman grope his way to the couch and sink down on it, sit there with his legs spread and his hands hanging down between his thighs.

"No," he said to the floor, his voice empty of emotion, "Verna don't know. I told her the place was locked up and I couldn't get in. She thinks he slipped on the rug, drunk, after she left . . . an accident like everybody else thought. I didn't kill him, not on purpose, but I guess you won't believe it."

"What happened that night, Joe?"

"Verna wasn't home when I got back. Her car was there, but she wasn't. I started to go out and look for her, and there she was on the road. She tried to tell me she'd been out for a walk, but it was past ten; she never went out walking that late. I knew she'd been with somebody; it was written all over her."

"So you beat it out of her that it was Dennison."

"Smacked her once, that's all it took. It wasn't the first time she cheated on me, she's a goddamn tramp, but that night . . . I don't know, I was tired from all the driving after a lousy hunting trip and I was so mad I couldn't see straight. I got in the truck and drove over here. I wasn't gonna do anything to Dennison, just tell him to keep his paws off my wife. Only they'd been boozing it up and he was smart-ass drunk; he laughed and called me a couple names, called Verna names. I got in his face, told him to shut his dirty mouth. Then . . . he took a wild swing at me, I shoved him, and next thing I know he's got a poker in his hand ready to take another swing at me with that. Wasn't anything I could do but belt him one."

"The contusion on his cheekbone," Runyon said.

"Yeah. The rug slipped and he went down and the back of his head slammed into the hearthstones and he was dead. Just like that, dead." Meeker raised his head to look at Rittenhouse. "Self-defense, Deputy. I swear to God I wouldn't of punched him if he hadn't picked up that poker."

"Then you should have reported what happened right away," Rittenhouse said, "told it just the way you did now."

"I was scared to. Only the two of us there, and Verna knew how pissed I was when I left home. You wouldn't of believed it was self-defense. Nobody would." His head drooped again, loose on the stem of his neck. "You don't now. Neither of you."

"You shouldn't have tried to cover it up."

"I couldn't think of nothing else to do. Crossbar leaning against the wall give me the idea. I didn't know if the trick'd work or not, but it didn't take long to get a nail and hammer out of my truck and try it." Long, shaky breath. "I wish to Christ it hadn't worked."

Rittenhouse asked, "Why did you come in

next morning with that lie about seeing the body through the window? You could have just kept quiet and let Hansen find what was left of Dennison next time he came up."

"I figured I had to, to make sure Verna kept her mouth shut."

"Figured it before you left here that night," Runyon said. "All the other window shutters were closed — Dennison left them that way. You opened the ones on the side window."

"Yeah. But I didn't know you couldn't see where the body was laying from outside or I'd of moved the couch or something. Didn't know it until a few minutes ago."

Rittenhouse said, "So you didn't plan to bring Fred and me out here when sun on the glass made it hard to see inside."

"No. I never thought about that. If you'd been able to see clear that morning I'd of been screwed then, I guess."

"That's right, you would have."

"Don't matter. I'm screwed now."

Meeker sat slumped and desolate as the deputy handcuffed him and read him his rights. Runyon thought that the little man's account of Tuesday night's events was probably true, felt almost sorry for him. Almost. He saved his compassion for the victims —

for Patricia Dennison when he told her how and why her husband had died.

15

I usually confine business matters to weekdays, reserving weekends for quality time with Kerry and Emily. But on this Saturday morning, with no family plans scheduled, I bit the bullet, so to speak, and went to meet Alex Chavez at SFPD's pistol range at Lake Merced for some long-overdue target practice.

Long overdue in my case, that is. Chavez, a diligent as well as a first-rate field operative, went frequently to the range to hone his skills; he had urged me to join him because he knew I'd been putting off the task. Despite forty-some years of familiarity with firearms, and an understanding of the necessity for them by those of us involved in law enforcement, I have an inherent aversion to guns. I've had too much firsthand experience with the ravages of gun violence, and the monstrous mass killings that have taken place with increasing regularity over the past several years sicken me even more. Still, I owed it to my family as well as to myself to remain as proficient with a handgun as possible at my age, should the occasion ever arise when I would need to use my .38 Colt Bodyguard again.

Another reason I gave in to Alex's urging was because I owed my life to him and his prowess with a handgun. At the close of a case we'd worked on together not so long ago, he'd got off a quick shot in poor light just in time to keep a vicious attack dog from tearing my throat out — a harrowing sequence that had disturbed my sleep for some time afterward. I wondered if it disturbed his as well. Neither of us had spoken of the incident since.

Chavez was waiting when I arrived at the range, all smiles as usual. He was that rarity in today's world, a genuinely happy man who loved his job. He'd joined the sheriff's department down in El Centro as soon as he was of age, married a woman he adored and who adored him in return, fathered three good kids, moved the family to San Francisco when the opportunity to join a private security firm came up. Some racially challenged individuals had a tendency to underestimate a short, stocky, perpetually smiling, slow-moving Hispanic. Actually, he was quick thinking, fast-moving when the situation called for it, and, like Jake Runyon, unflappable in a crisis.

Technically the range is open only to police personnel and investigators attached to the D.A.'s office. Civilians are allowed when accompanied by an officer, but that restriction doesn't apply to authorized private investigators and security people. You need to make an appointment to secure a target range, especially on Saturdays, which Chavez and I had done. Even so, we had to wait a while before we could take our turns. The place was crowded as usual, and noisy even with Peltor earmuffs in place.

Alex and I each fired upward of fifty rounds. His score of close-grouping hits at various distances was near perfect. As for mine . . .

"You're definitely a little rusty, amigo," he said when we were done.

"More than a little," I said ruefully. "My hand's still pretty steady, but my eye isn't what it used to be."

"You need to get out here more often, you don't mind my saying so."

"No argument there. You have permission to kick my butt next time you suggest it and I find an excuse to say no."

He grinned. "Figuratively or literally?"

"I'll leave that up to you."

I offered to buy him lunch and he accepted. There's a restaurant at the Lake Merced Golf Club nearby, but you need to be a member or with a member to eat there. I would not have felt comfortable in its rarified surroundings anyway. I know that millions of people are passionate golfers, but it's a game that has no appeal whatsoever for me. Baseball and pro football are my sports, the former much more than the latter now that the 49ers have abandoned San Francisco for Santa Clara forty-three miles south, a move made strictly to feed the greed of one of the NFL's worst owners.

We went out to the Beach Chalet on the Great Highway. Crowded there, too, thanks to the good weather, and we had to wait for a table. Worth it, though; the food there is always good. Companionable shoptalk and a second round of draft beer lengthened the meal, so that it was after one when Chavez and I parted company and I headed home.

I got to the condo just as the mailman was delivering two cartons of books to Kerry — the promised trade paperback editions of Cybil's collected works. I carried them inside, put them on the table in the dining room. While she went to get a knife, I stood looking at the cartons — and my memory jogged and I remembered the padded mailing bag that James Cahill had briefly lifted from his missing wife's desk. Copies of her latest novel, he'd said. No reason I should remember that, out of the blue like this . . . or was there?

I was mentally hunting for one when Kerry came back. Her excitement as we opened the cartons prodded the memory fragment back into the compartment that had disgorged it.

We'd seen cover proofs of the five "Cybil Wade writing as Samuel Leatherman" books, and the finished copies were even more appealing. For the collections, the publisher had used full-color reproductions of forties pulp covers that had prominently featured the Leatherman pseudonym; for the two Max Ruffe novels, new pulp-style artwork had been commissioned that was substantially superior to the bland dust jacket illustrations on the original hardcover editions of *Dead Eye* and *Black Eye.* Kerry was ecstatic. She fondled a copy of each book, opened each to page through it and to sniff its newness. After which she carried the five editions into her office and arranged them, covers facing outward, on the shelf containing Cybil's author's copies. This made the shelf, already a kind of shrine to the mother Kerry had adored, even more of a riot of color than the ones in my study that contained the six thousand pulp magazines I'd accumulated since I began collecting them as a teenager.

For the time being we stored the rest of the contributors' copies in her office closet. Some would be sent to Cybil's friends in Redwood Village and the last surviving pulp writer she'd known in the old days, Waldo Ramsey, a minor contributor who had shared the contents pages of three issues of *Midnight Detective* with her. They'd kept in touch by letter — he still preferred a typewriter to a computer, as had she. He was in his nineties now and as mentally sharp as ever; he would appreciate having the collected volumes.

Tamara called on my cell a few minutes past four. From the agency, where she admitted to having already put in nearly eight hours of work.

"How come?" I asked. "Why didn't you take the day off?"

"Why do you think? Crap keeps piling up on my desk and somebody's got to deal with it."

Grouchy Tamara today. Fortunately, that's

one of her least common personas; the more pleasant, if not downright sunny, versions take precedence. Another setback in the ongoing soap opera of her love life, maybe. But I knew better than to bring up the subject. If I did, I was liable to get the most unpleasant persona of all, Pit Bull Tamara.

"You could hire another techie to help out," I said. "The agency can afford it."

"Yeah, well, then I'd have to teach her or him what to do and that'd take more time than it's worth. I've got my own system; you know that. Somebody new would probably screw it up. Better if I just slog my way through on my own."

"Okay. You know best."

"Oh, sure. Sometimes I think I don't know a damn thing."

"Wait until you get to be my age. Then you'll *know* you don't know a damn thing."

She muttered something I didn't catch. Then, "I did some more digging for you on the people in the Cahill case. Found out something about one of 'em I thought you'd want to know."

"Which one?"

"Dr. Paul Nesbitt."

"Important?"

"How do I know if it's important or not? You're the detective; I'm just the office drudge."

Oh, boy. "You're the glue that holds everything together and you know it. Go ahead; let's hear what you've got."

"Dude's a good physician but crappy human being."

"Oh?"

"Nurse at the clinic where he worked before he went with Prime Medical filed a sexual harassment suit against him."

That was something of an eyebrow raiser. "How long ago?"

"Three years. No specific evidence to support the claim, so it didn't damage his medical career. Whole thing was hushed up. But there was enough fire for the nurse, Carolyn Feeney, to get a five K settlement out of him."

"How do you know that? Settlement terms are usually kept private —"

"I talked to her, that's how. On the phone a little while ago. Got lucky and caught her at home. She says she wasn't the doc's only victim. That he's a sexual predator, the charm-and-bullshit kind."

"Can she back that up?"

"No. The one other woman she knows that he hassled was too afraid to come forward."

"Ms. Feeney's still bitter, still angry?"

"Yeah, and I don't blame her. Men like him ought to be deballed along with rapists and child molesters."

"They're not quite in the same class —"

"How would you know? You ever been sexually harassed?"

As a matter of fact, I had been — once. But I was not about to get into that with Tamara. It hadn't been much of an incident, and while I hated to admit it, in a perverse way I'd found it uncomfortably flattering. Aging-male reaction; for a woman of any age, unwelcome sexual advances are neither flattering nor justifiable.

I said, "Sounds as though she was eager to talk about the experience. Are you sure referring to him as a sexual predator wasn't just ax-grinding on her part?"

"Hard to be sure over the phone, but I think she was being straight with me. Telling it like it was."

"What did you say to her about our interest in Nesbitt?"

"Routine inquiry on a case he was peripherally involved in."

"But not a sexual harassment case."

"No. Hey, don't sweat it, okay? I know what I'm doing. You taught me real good, boss man."

Except that every now and then she could

be intemperate, particularly when she was in a mood like this one. But her judgment had improved considerably over time, and she hadn't given me cause not to trust it in a long while.

"Okay," I said. "As long as you're satisfied that she won't use the inquiry in any way that calls attention to us."

"She won't. Settlement terms won't let her. She doesn't want anything more to do with him. So? Important?"

"Hard to say. But I'm glad you dug it up."

"Yeah, well, important or not, I still say any son of a bitch who sexually harasses women ought to have his nuts cut off."

The second call on my cell came a few minutes before seven. Kerry and Emily were in the kitchen, whipping up some mystery dinner that somebody at the Bates and Carpenter ad agency had recommended to Kerry, and I was lying on the living room couch rereading one of Cybil's Max Ruffe pulp novelettes and listening to jazz.

I like most kinds of music, except for the atonal, teeth-grinding kind like rap, but jazz has always been my favorite. All kinds, with a slight preference for the old New Orleans style — stomps, rags, cannonballs, blues — of Armstrong, Ellington, Beiderbecke,

Count Basie, Kid Ory. Tonight it was the lighter, smoother variety produced by Stan Kenton — good, relaxing background music for reading. I had the volume on the CD player Emily had given me for my birthday turned down fairly low; otherwise I wouldn't have heard the phone's ringtone. As it was, the thing must have gone off two or three times before it penetrated through the earbuds.

The call was from a number I didn't recognize. Robo junk call at this time on a Saturday evening? It had happened before; the relentlessness of some telemarketers and their ilk is exceeded only by that of politicians hunting campaign contributions. The reason I answered instead of letting it go to hang-up or voice mail was because the number had a 520 East Bay prefix.

An unfamiliar male voice said my name interrogatively, I responded with a cautious affirmation, half-expecting a pitch of some kind, and he said, "My name is Carl Moxon, of Blount and Moxon in Walnut Creek. Sorry to be calling at this hour, but it's rather important."

"I'm not familiar with Blount and Moxon."

"We're a law firm. I am James Cahill's attorney."

That got my attention, hoisted me upright on the couch. "Yes, Mr. Moxon?"

"I'm calling at his request, to apprise you of recent developments in the matter of his wife's disappearance. He is allowed only one phone call, as you know, so he was not able to contact you directly."

Lawyers. Never say anything straight out, always bob and weave at the edges. "Are you telling me he's been arrested?"

"Yes. I just came from conferring with him at the Contra Costa County Jail. Inasmuch as you have been investigating on his behalf, he instructed me to acquaint you with the details."

"Arrested on what charge?"

"Homicide. The murder of his wife."

Damn. "So she's been found. Where? When?"

"Early yesterday, near a nature preserve east of Martinez."

"How long had she been there?"

"The state of decomposition indicates several days."

"Since Cahill reported her missing?"

"So it would seem. The police believe she was killed at her home, the remains then carried away that night or the following day and, for want of a better word, dumped."

"Cause of death?"

"Apparently a blow or blows to the head with her laptop computer."

Some murder weapon. "Found in the same place as the body?"

"Together with it, yes. It was the means of identification of the victim. That, and an inscription on her wedding ring."

"Who found the body?"

"Evidently a passerby or someone on a nature walk."

"Evidently?"

"The person placed an anonymous call to the county sheriff's department," Moxon said. "People nowadays are loath to become involved in unpleasant situations, as I'm sure you know."

"Who's in charge of the investigation? The sheriff?"

"In conjunction with Lieutenant Frank Kowalski of the Walnut Creek police. Kowalski has your name. He wants to talk to you, so you can expect to hear from him soon."

"All right."

"Are you in possession of any information pertinent to Mr. Cahill's defense? If so, you'll need to share it with me as well as Lieutenant Kowalski."

"I wish I did, but I don't. What does Cahill say?"

"That he's innocent, of course. That he loved his wife and would never have harmed her. He seemed quite broken up by the news of her death." No compassion in Moxon's voice. Just statements of fact in an unemotional monotone.

"Do you believe him?"

"What I believe if of no consequence. I won't be representing him in this matter — I am not a criminal attorney. But of course I'll see to it that he receives the best possible counsel for his defense. Whoever that is will want to confer with you, I'm sure, particularly if you accede to Mr. Cahill's plea."

"What plea?"

"The primary reason he insisted I contact you. His exact words were: 'Tell him I swear to God I didn't do it. Tell him he's my only hope.' "

16

Saturday morning. Back on the road again, heading home.

Home. Funny. For most of his life his home had been Seattle. Born and raised there, his father a fireman, his mother a grade-school teacher. The bulk of his memories were from there, the good intermingled with the bad. Joining the police force, working his way up in the ranks; the birth of his son; the fractious years with Andrea; the long, hard hours riding in patrol cars before and after his promotion to detective; working vice in the Pike's Market area downtown before the city cleaned it up, then the robbery detail in the crime-infested areas of West Seattle and the railyards and terminal along the East Waterway and the Duwamish Waterway; the pursuit accident that had killed Ron Cain and screwed up his leg and forced him to quit the PD rather than accept a desk job; the years learning the private investigative trade with Caldwell & Associates; and Colleen, most of all the long too-short, too–soon gone years with the only woman he'd ever loved, all that they'd shared, the contentment that had transformed so suddenly into pain and fear and then the core of grief that still burned deep inside him.

All those mixed memories, still vivid, followed by the scant few since his move to San Francisco, those too good and bad, the inability to reconnect with Joshua, the difficult cases he'd worked for and with Bill and Tamara, the loneliness, the lengthy affair with another damaged individual that brought salvation to both him and Bryn and then the inevitable separation that had left him alone again except for his work. Then why should he consider San Francisco to be home now? This new place, this city just as empty and non-nurturing as Seattle had become? And yet he did. For some reason he couldn't explain, whenever he left for a period of time he now thought of returning to San Francisco as going home.

Originally he'd intended to leave Eagle Lake the night before. But the whole afternoon had been taken up with the Joe Meeker business — an official statement to

213

be prepared and signed; interrogation of a not very upset Verna Meeker to get her account that Rittenhouse had asked him to sit in on; a repeat of explanations to the sheriff who'd arrived to haul Meeker off to the county jail, there being only two small holding cells at the Eagle Lake substation. When it was all over and done with, it was after 5:30 and he was tired and hungry. He'd politely declined Rittenhouse's invitation to dinner at his home — peopled out and in no mood for socializing, even in payment for what the deputy considered a favor — and gone back to the lodge.

By the time he finished eating, reading a pair of e-mails from Tamara, and dodging his way through a telephone conversation with Patricia Dennison, he had none of his usual desire for a long road trip without a night's rest. And his room had already been paid for.

Tamara had tentatively IDed the woman whose first name Lloyd Hansen had provided: Lucia Dinucci, owner of the Superior Lingerie Shop on Post Street near Union Square. There didn't seem to be much doubt that she was Philip Dennison's mistress, but Runyon was thorough to a fault; he needed to make absolutely sure. That was one reason he hadn't given the client

Lucia Dinucci's name; the other was the background info Tamara had provided on Patricia Dennison. He also hadn't told Mrs. Dennison about her husband's involvement with Verna Meeker or the manner in which he'd died; that was better done in person. He'd arranged to meet her at her home this afternoon — no specific time. Would he know then who her husband's lover was? He might, he said, but he wasn't sure.

That was the thing: he wasn't sure yet if he was going to give her Lucia Dinucci's name.

Patricia Dennison was less of an enigma now, but what Tamara had found out about her was not particularly reassuring. Born and raised in Portland, Oregon, the only child of lower-middle-class parents. Attended Reed College on an art scholarship for three years, where she provided sketches to and also wrote poetry for the school's literary magazine. Dropped out in her fourth year because she'd gotten pregnant by a fellow student who refused to marry her, then either lost or aborted the fetus, it wasn't clear which. The experience had had a severe emotional effect on her, caused a breakdown that required short-term hospitalization. A series of menial jobs afterward, barely making ends meet, until she met and married Philip Dennison, who was then employed by a Portland firm. The marriage considerably improved her financial situation, particularly after her husband landed his new, much higher-paying sales position with the San Francisco software company. No children. No close friends. No indication that she had resumed her study of or interest in art.

Portrait of a damaged, likely bitter, self-contained woman with no marketable skills, who liked living well after the privations of her early years and preferred marriage to a cheating husband to giving up her expensive home and comfortable lifestyle. That much was clear. What still wasn't clear, now that the cheating husband was dead, was whether or not she was capable of an act of violence toward a rival who, in her view, was at least partially responsible for turning her carefully structured existence upside down and creating an uncertain future.

So Runyon still faced a moral dilemma. He had a professional obligation to fulfill, and he did not like lying to or withholding information from a client. Mrs. Dennison just wanted to talk to the woman, she'd said, and probably that was true. Probably. But given her background, she might possess a hidden desire for revenge, might be capable of acting on it. He had no guarantee that a single face-to-face confrontation that he stood witness to, no matter how it went, would be the end of it. Rittenhouse had been right. If any harm came to Lucia Dinucci, even any attempted harm, at the hands of Patricia Dennison, Runyon would be morally, if not legally, responsible.

The problem had bothered him last night and it bothered him now as he drove. He still hadn't made up his mind what to do. And wouldn't until after he spoke to Lucia Dinucci and then kept his afternoon appointment with Patricia Dennison.

The Superior Lingerie Shop was a small storefront with two show windows flanking the front door. Both windows contained manikins, one modeling lacy red bra and panties, the other a see-through nightgown. Inside there were displays of underwear, foundation garments, negligees, nightgowns, peignoirs, and a variety of accessories, not all of the sexy type. The kind of place that catered to a general and discerning clientele.

There were no customers when Runyon walked in, no one except a willowy, thirty-ish woman behind the sales counter. Hansen had described Dennison's lady friend as good-looking and having "silky black hair, olive complexion, great legs." This woman qualified on all counts, the "great legs" part evident when she stepped out smiling from behind the counter and approached him. The floral-design dress she wore, while not being particularly provocative overall, was fashioned so that the hem ended just above the knee.

"Yes, sir," she said. "May I help you?"

"You can if you're Lucia Dinucci."

"I am. May I ask how you know my name?"

Instead of answering the question, Runyon said, "I understand you're a friend of Philip Dennison."

He watched her closely as he spoke. How she reacted would determine how much further he'd go, just how much he would tell her. If she denied it —

But she didn't. The smile faded, drawing coral-tinted lips into a straight line. An emotion he couldn't quite read darkened luminous black eyes. She said slowly, "Did he give you my name?"

"No."

"Then why did you mention him?"

"*Are* you a friend of his, Ms. Dinucci?"

"I was," she said. Now the emotion was clearer: a combination of sadness and hurt. "Not anymore. Why do you want to know?

Who are you?"

"My name is Runyon," he said, and showed her his ID.

She looked at it, then closed her eyes and backed up a step. When she looked at him again, she said with no inflection, "I suppose you're employed by his wife."

"Yes, as a matter of fact."

"Well, you can tell her she has nothing more to worry about. Nothing whatsoever." Lucia Dinucci's lower lip trembled slightly. "She never did, really."

"How long have you known the man?"

"It doesn't matter. Not anymore."

"I'd still like to know."

"A little over a year. He came in one day to buy a negligee . . . a present for a lady friend, he said. You can believe this or not, but I didn't know until much later that he was married. If I had, I would not have gotten involved with him."

Runyon was silent.

"By the time I found out, we'd already —" She shook her head, turned abruptly, and went back behind the sales counter. Runyon followed her. "It's over; I ended it," she said then. "That's all that matters."

"When did you end it? Last week?"

"Yes, last week."

"In person or on the phone?"

"What difference does that make?"

"You were supposed to meet him at Eagle Lake, spend a few days there with him, but you changed your mind. Is that right?"

". . . Yes. How did you know that?"

"Why did you change your mind?"

"Because I couldn't . . . I couldn't go up there again, be with him anymore. I thought I loved him, he made me believe he loved me, but it was all a lie, all so . . . cheap. I don't suppose you understand, but . . . I started to pack and I couldn't and that was when I stopped lying to myself."

"You told him it was over when he called you that night?"

"You know about that, too? Yes, that's when I told him. He was very angry. Very angry. I think he'd been drinking." She shook her head again. "I don't want anything more to do with Phil Dennison. That is God's honest truth. Tell his wife that. Tell her he's all hers."

"He's not all hers," Runyon said. "He's nobody's anymore."

"I don't . . . What do you mean?"

Lucia Dinucci had made a favorable impression on him — the old, old story of a decent woman who'd made the mistake of falling in love with the wrong man. She had a right to know that he was no longer among the living. Better the news should come from him than from Patricia Dennison, no matter what he decided to do about her.

"Philip Dennison is dead," he said. "He was killed at Eagle Lake last Tuesday night."

She closed her eyes again. Otherwise she stood very still, her hands closed at her sides. Several seconds crept away before she said in a small, dull voice, "How?"

Runyon said, "You could call it an accident."

"What kind of accident?"

"It might be better if we just left it at that."

"No. Please. I want to know."

Before he could respond, the bell over the door jangled and a woman in a dark green suit came in, went straight to a display of silken underwear. Immediately Lucia Dinucci stepped around the counter, crossed the shop in measured strides, and said something to the woman that Runyon couldn't hear. The customer said irritably, "All right, then, I'll just go somewhere else," and went out. Ms. Dinucci closed the door behind her, hung a **Closed** sign in its glass panel.

"Please," she said again when she came back to Runyon. "How did Philip die?"

He told her, keeping it brief, sparing her

some but not all of the sordid details. If she was dismayed by the fact that Dennison had died because he'd been shacked up with a married waitress he'd picked up on the rebound, she gave no outward indication of it.

After a time she said, "He'd still be alive if I'd kept our date."

"You have no cause to blame yourself."

"I know that. I was just stating a fact." Pause. "I'm sorry he's dead and I'm sorry for his wife, but I'm not sorry I ended our affair the way I did. Does that sound callous?"

"No," he said truthfully, "it doesn't."

"He could be funny, charming, exciting to be with." Talking to herself now as much as to him. "But at some level I think I knew all along, even before I found out he was married, that he wasn't really the good, kind man he pretended to be."

Runyon didn't respond. But he was thinking that she was right: Philip Dennison had not been a good man at all, and she had realized it in time to save herself even greater heartache. She was far better off with him gone from her life. And so was Patricia Dennison, whether she accepted that fact or not.

17

JAKE RUNYON

The Dennison home was a second-floor flat in a large, old-style stucco building in the lower southern corner of the Presidio, not far from Letterman Army Medical Center and the approach to the Golden Gate Bridge. Street parking in this neighborhood, as in the Marina District nearby, was at its usual premium; Runyon had to drive around for ten minutes before he finally found a spot two blocks away. It was a warm afternoon; it felt good to get out and stretch his legs a little after all the driving.

Patricia Dennison buzzed him in as soon as he rang her bell. Waiting impatiently for his arrival; one look at her when she opened the door confirmed it. She wore a dark blue outfit with a yellow scarf at the throat — no mourning clothes for her. Her dark blond hair was neatly combed, her makeup carefully applied. None of this was for him. She was the type of woman who would always dress with care and casual elegance, no matter what the occasion. Always, even on the grim mission to Eagle Lake.

"I expected you much sooner than this, Mr. Runyon."

"Sorry. I couldn't get here any earlier."

"Have you anything to tell me?"

"Some things, yes."

"Well?"

"Suppose we sit down first."

The cornflower-blue eyes probed his, as if she was trying to read his mind. Then she turned and led him into a wide living room. Modern furnishings — big, horseshoe-shaped sofa in some sort of nubby cream-colored fabric, matching chairs, low black tables, white rugs on a hardwood floor, white drapes with black accents drawn open over windows that gave an oblique view of the Golden Gate Bridge. Framed black-and-white still-life sketches of mammals and birds on the walls; too professionally detailed to be hers, he judged, though he didn't know enough about art to be sure. The only color in the room was from some red throw pillows on the couch, the bases and shades of a pair of arty table lamps. Everything was as well arranged and as tidy as Patricia Dennison herself.

The contour chair she directed him to looked comfortable and was. She went to the sofa, but before she sat down she said, "Do you know the woman's name?"

"I know who your husband was with before he died. Verna Meeker, a waitress at the Lakefront Café."

Now she sat down, smoothing her skirt over her thighs. "A waitress," she repeated. "A pickup when his mistress canceled, I suppose."

"Yes."

"Attractive?"

"Some men might think so."

She said sardonically, "I thought Philip had better taste."

Runyon said nothing.

"Was he shacked up with her the entire time?"

"Not exactly. She lives in the next cabin down the road from Lloyd Hansen's. Her husband was away on a hunting trip. Joe Meeker, a local handyman."

"I see."

"But Meeker came back earlier than expected on Tuesday night. Caught her as she was returning home, beat the truth out of her, then went storming to the Hansen cabin to confront your husband."

"He was there when Philip died?"

"More than that," Runyon said. "There was an argument. According to Meeker, your husband was about to hit him with a poker, he retaliated with a punch, and that was when your husband slipped and fell against the hearthstone."

It took a few seconds for her to process that. "So this . . . handyman was responsible for Philip's death."

"Yes. He was afraid he'd be blamed for it, so he tried to cover up by creating the illusion that the cabin was sealed. If you want to know how he did that —"

"I don't, no. I don't care what he did or how he did it. Or how you found out about it. Has he been arrested?"

"And charged with manslaughter, yes."

"Philip died because he was fucking some tramp and her husband attacked him." The four-letter word sounded even more out of place in these genteel surroundings than it had when she'd used it in the car on the drive to Eagle Lake. "My God. I wish you hadn't told me."

"If I hadn't, Deputy Rittenhouse would have."

"All right. So now you've done your duty."

"It's difficult to come to terms with, I know —"

"No, you don't. You don't know at all.

How could you? You didn't know Philip; you weren't married to him for ten years."

He had nothing to say to that.

She misinterpreted his silence. "You're thinking that I didn't know him, either. Well, you're right, I didn't. Not anywhere near as well as I thought I did."

Still nothing to say.

"I knew he was weak and deceitful, a typical male who shunned his marriage vows when an opportunity presented itself. I hated it, but I made allowances and learned to live with it. It's hard enough dealing with his death, but this . . . this —"

Abruptly she stood, skirted the sofa to the window where she stood staring out. Runyon remained silent. Even if he'd had words that might offer some comfort, which he didn't, she would not have wanted to hear them. Not from him. Not from anyone, most likely. Her reaction to the news had reinforced his take on her character: a self-contained unit, one who kept her emotions tightly in check.

The silence seemed to grow. If there had been a clock in the room, its ticking would have assumed overloud proportions. That kind of silence.

It must have been nearly five minutes before she turned to face him again. Her hands were folded together at her waist, her mouth and jaw set in taut lines. Runyon knew what she was going to say before she said it.

"What about the other woman? The one he went up there to meet, the one who stood him up?"

"Does it matter now?"

"It does to me. Do you know who she is?"

He had already made his decision. Lying to a client, misleading a client, still went strongly against his grain, but there were times when you felt you had just cause to compromise your standards. This was one of them.

"Not yet, no," he said.

"But you'll be able to find out."

"I don't think so. Or that I want to."

Her mouth tightened even more. "What kind of answer is that? It's what you were hired to do."

"Not so. Not part of the original agreement."

"You promised me you'd find her."

"No, I didn't. I said I'd try."

"You're splitting hairs —"

"Let me ask you a question, Mrs. Dennison. Do you still feel the need to confront the woman?"

"Yes."

"Why?"

"I told you before, I have some things to say to her."

"What things, exactly?"

"That's none of your business."

"Berate her? Accuse her? Call her names?"

"I told you —"

"See what she looks like, what kind of woman your husband found so appealing? Then, if she doesn't measure up, salvage your pride by feeling superior to her?"

She came away from the window, stopped in front of his chair to glare down at him. "You have no right to talk to me that way."

"Did I strike a nerve?"

"No, you did not."

Yes, he had. He could see it in her face. But he couldn't tell if there was more to it than that, if some sort of revenge was also what she was after. No use trying. There was just no way to know for certain what went on inside somebody else's head.

"Do you also intend to confront Verna Meeker?"

". . . What?"

"The married waitress your husband was shacked up with. You have things to say to her, too?"

"I . . ." The question had caught her off guard, taken her aback.

"Do you?"

"She's just a cheap tramp. The other one . . ."

"You don't think she's a cheap tramp, too?"

"No, I don't. I think she must be —"

"A decent woman who made the mistake of getting involved with a married man? Suppose that's who and what she is. What then?"

She backed away from him. "I don't like you, Mr. Runyon. You're . . . impertinent."

"I don't sugarcoat the facts as I see them, if that's what you mean."

"I ought to file a complaint against you with your agency."

"That's your prerogative. Do you want me to leave now?"

"Are you going to find Philip's mistress or aren't you?"

"No, ma'am, I'm not. I've done the job I was hired to do. As far as I'm concerned, that concludes our business."

"I'll get another detective, then. The telephone book is full of them."

"Also your prerogative," Runyon said. "But I'd think twice about it if I were you."

She retreated another step. The backs of her knees bumped against the coffee table, stopping her, making her wince.

"Take my advice, Mrs. Dennison. Bury your husband; bury the past along with him. Save yourself any more grief."

Six-beat. Then she said, "Damn you," but there was no heat in the words and she was no longer glaring. "Go on, leave. Leave me alone."

He did what she asked — went to the door and let himself out, left her alone with her anger, her bitterness, her feelings of loss and betrayal: the same feelings she must have had when the college man who'd gotten her pregnant abandoned her. Maybe she'd heed his advice; maybe she wouldn't. For Lucia Dinucci's sake as well as hers, he hoped she would.

Out of his hands now in any event. And he still felt he'd made the right decision.

18

A lot of ex-cops and other civilians in law enforcement jobs work Sundays, but I'm not one of them. Never on Sunday, that's my motto. Of course mottos, like rules, are made to be broken, and every now and then I've had cause to break mine. I had no such specific cause on this Sunday, but I worked part of it just the same. Could not have stopped myself if I'd wanted to.

I brooded Saturday evening after the lawyer Moxon's phone call, to the point where it cost me some sleep. And I kept right on brooding Sunday morning. What kept plaguing my mind was not only Cahill's arrest but also the brutality of Alice Cahill's murder and disposal of her body. I had never met the woman, it had seemed probable all along that she would not turn up alive after being missing for more than a week, and yet her death depressed me. The last few years of her short life had been filled with tragedy and despair — the car accident that claimed a stranger's life, the resultant agoraphobia, the paranoia and sudden mood swings. She'd been a plagiarist, yes, but even that may have been attributable to her damaged psyche. No matter how flawed she'd been, she had deserved a better fate.

One more shattered life among the many I'd come across in my work. One more victim. All of them combined made for a heavy burden. Ghosts are supposed to be ethereal, but not mine. Mine had substance and weight, and the capacity to inflict psychic pain.

Cahill, I was convinced, was also a victim. Of circumstances, of misapprehension. I'd dealt with plenty of his type, too, over the years, and you get so you can recognize them for what they are: pawns, scapegoats, the unjustly accused. I felt sorry for him, sorry as hell, but what could I do about it?

Something, maybe. Make an effort, at least.

I'd heard nothing from the Walnut Creek cop, Lieutenant Kowalski; obviously he felt a statement from me could wait until the start of the workweek because there was little, if anything, of importance I could tell him. I considered trying to contact him, but even if he was on duty today and available it wouldn't buy me anything. He would not supply me with details. Why should he? As far as he and the Contra Costa County sheriff's department were concerned, they had the guilty party in custody.

As far as I was concerned, they were wrong.

The case against James Cahill did not feel right to me.

Gut instinct. Based partly on my conversations with the man, my impressions and perceptions of him, and partly on the facts as Moxon had related them to me. But there were more in his possession that he hadn't related and I hadn't asked for.

He had given me his cell phone number. I called it, half-expecting it to go to voice mail, but he answered almost immediately. "Something you forgot to tell me last night?" he asked when I identified myself.

"No. A few more questions."

"Can't they wait?" Now he sounded a little irritated. "I just arrived at Diablo Hills and my foursome has a ten o'clock tee time."

Typical lawyer. More interested in playing golf than in discussing a client in jail on a homicide charge. The only thing men like him preferred to a golf club in hand was a four- or five-figure check.

"This won't take long. You told me Alice Cahill's body was discovered near the nature preserve east of Martinez. How remote is that area?"

"Why do you want to know that?"

"Just answer the question please, Mr. Moxon."

He said snippily, "Not particularly remote. The nature preserve is close to Highway 680, off the road to Avon."

Avon. Unincorporated area on the way to Port Chicago. "Near the preserve, you said. Not inside it."

"No. Off a dirt track beyond the entrance."

"Within sight of the Avon road?"

"Fairly close to it. In a shallow gully behind a screen of trees."

"Just dumped there, no attempt made to bury it?"

"Dumped in haste, evidently."

"Because of the proximity to the road."

"Presumably."

"Wrapped in something — blanket, drop cloth?"

"Large trash bags," Moxon said distastefully, "bound with duct tape. The bags were torn, the remains . . . damaged by small animals."

"And the computer was inside the bags."

"Yes."

"Was anything else found in the gully?"

"Not that I was informed of."

"The anonymous call. Male or female?"

"They couldn't be sure. A deep voice, but muffled."

"No trace on the number?"

"No. The call was probably made from a prepaid cell phone. Look, I don't see the point of these questions —"

"There's a point," I said. "Any chance of you getting me an audience with Mr. Cahill?"

"Not immediately, if at all. No one but legal counsel is permitted to see him until after his arraignment."

"Which is when?"

"Tomorrow afternoon."

"Will you see what you can do and let me know?"

"Yes, but don't count on permission being granted."

"Do you have a criminal attorney for him yet?"

"Hardly. This is the weekend, after all." There were noises in the background now, raised voice and laughter; he was probably inside the country club. "Now I really must go or I'll be late," he said. "I'll notify you of any relevant developments, so I'd appreciate it if you wouldn't call me again unless absolutely necessary."

Jerk. Or, as Tamara would say, asshole.

I sat there in my study, working my brain again. Now I *really* did not like the case against James Cahill.

The main reason was the dumping of the body. The only conceivable explanation for Cahill having done that, and for including the murder weapon and leaving Alice Cahill's wedding ring on her finger, was blind panic. But if my take on his character was correct, and I believed it was, he was not the type to panic in a crisis. His love for his wife had survived the agoraphobia, her mood swings and panic attacks, his sexual deprivation; no matter what the Nesbitts believed, I did not see him as capable of bludgeoning her to death in a rage, drunken or otherwise. If he'd killed her, it would have been accidentally, an act of self-defense. And afterward he would have been horrified at what he'd done, and remorseful, and he'd have called the police and owned up.

Then there was the anonymous call. Moxon's explanation that it had been made by someone who did not want to become involved in a murder investigation was supportable enough. But I'm always leery of anonymous calls in such cases as these, especially those that can't be traced back to their source. The timing was also too convenient to suit me.

And then there was the location of the body, a shallow gully where it had apparently lain undetected for a week. On my laptop I looked up a Google map of the general area. The nature preserve, Waterbird Regional Preserve, was in a semi-remote location, yes. But why had the body been dumped there, only a short distance off the Avon road with no attempt at burial or concealment? Another thing: the place was approximately a forty-five-minute drive from Cahill's home in Shelter Hills Estates. Why risk traveling that distance when there were more isolated rural areas much closer to Walnut Creek, places where a body could be hidden away for months, years?

Well, there was one good answer to all of those questions. The person who had killed Alice Cahill wanted the body to be discovered, expected it to be more or less immediately. That explained the chosen location, the presence of the laptop and wedding ring to ensure swift identification, the anonymous phone call after a week had gone by without discovery. All done in order to frame James Cahill for the crime.

All right, then — who?

And what was the motive for Alice Cahill's murder?

I called a halt to the brooding around noon and took Kerry and Emily to lunch at Cellini's Ristorante, one of the best Italian restaurants outside North Beach. It's on Taraval, out toward Sunset Boulevard, a small and unpretentious place that has been in the same family for three generations. Their specialty is Emily's favorite, old-world-style spaghetti and meatballs. The toasted garlic bread they serve with it is good, though my version, made with a generous blend of Parmigiano-Reggiano and Pecorino Romano cheeses, is better. The ladies' opinion, not just mine. Ah, but the spaghetti and meatballs at Cellini's is *senza pari, fantastico.*

"This sauce is *so* good," Emily said as she dug in. "What do they put in it to make it taste like this?"

"They're not telling," Kerry said. "Secret family recipe."

"Put a bunch of ingredients in a pot," I said, "add a pinch of this and a dash of that, and let it simmer for a day or so. That's all there is to it."

"Hah. That's how we do it at home, Dad,

and it just doesn't come out like this."

"Well, we're not fine old-world chefs."

"We put in every herb and spice that's called for."

"Maybe we don't; maybe we leave something out."

"Like what?"

"I don't know, some little thing."

"It's always the little things," Kerry said philosophically. "We'll probably never know."

We went on eating. But then I stopped in mid-feed, put my fork down. "Little things," I said. "An accumulation of little things."

"Mmm?"

"What, Dad?"

"Essentially that's what pasta sauce, any complicated dish, is — an accumulation of little things. Right? Same is true of detective work sometimes. Only instead of meat and vegetables, herbs and spices, the ingredients are something you've seen or heard, some little fact you've learned, all tossed together in a mental pot. Let them simmer long enough, and eventually you'll end up with the right dish."

Kerry rolled her eyes. "That metaphor needs work."

"No, I'm serious. All you need to do is identify the little things one by one until you have the lot."

"Like a list of ingredients in a recipe," Emily said.

"Exactly."

"Are you just making a general observation," Kerry asked, "or does this have something to do with the Cahill matter?"

"It does. I have a feeling I've gathered enough bits and pieces to tell me who killed Alice Cahill and why. Maybe not enough to prove it, but enough to create reasonable doubt of Cahill's guilt."

"But you haven't identified them yet?"

"One or two. The rest will come."

"You hope."

"I hope. ASAP."

19

TAMARA

That fool Horace wouldn't stop pressuring her for an answer to his marriage proposal. Wouldn't let up for a minute every time they were together or talked on the phone the past few days.

"Come on, Tam, don't keep me hanging like this. Just say yes." Said that ten times if he said it once.

"I need more time to think it over."

"Why? You know we belong together. You know I love you."

"That's what you kept saying before you went to Philadelphia and hooked up with Mary from Rochester."

"Everybody makes a big mistake at least once in his life and Mary was mine. How many times, how many ways, can I say I'm sorry?"

"Only has to be once if you mean it."

"I do, honest I do. I was lonely back there;

that's my only excuse. And Mary was . . . well, available, convenient."

"Convenient! You almost married her."

"Her idea, not mine. She talked me into it. But I didn't go through with it because I couldn't."

"Sounded like you were damn eager to go through with it when you called me up and smacked me with the news."

"I guess I was, then. But I never loved Mary; I only thought I did, and not for long. You're the only woman I've ever loved."

"Lay that line on her, too? Tell her you loved her?"

"No. Never, not once. After I came to my senses I told her I loved *you.* That's why she broke it off."

"Should've broken it off while you were poking her with it."

"You don't mean that, Tam. You know you love me as much as I love you."

"I'm not so sure I know what love is."

"Great sex, for one thing. We light each other's fire every time."

"Same as you and Mary did?"

"Don't bring her up again, please. It's you and me I'm talking about. I've never had better sex and I'll bet you haven't, either. We're perfect together in bed."

"Nothing's perfect. And you can't build a

marriage on sex alone."

"No, but that's not all we have going for us. We like the same things, we have the same opinions, we can talk to each other, we're both willing to compromise —"

"Hah."

"Marry me, Tam. Just say yes!"

On and on like that. Friday night, Saturday morning, Saturday evening, Sunday morning. It was the pressure that had driven her to the agency for a full eight hours on Saturday, even though she'd just gotten her period and hadn't felt like working. If she'd stayed home he'd have hung around pushing and cajoling all day. She hadn't let him stay the night, but he called up first thing Sunday morning, not so subtly pressuring again, wanting to spend the day with her so he could do it some more. No way. She'd taken a bite out of him on the phone; if she let him come over and he started in again, as cramped as she was, she'd end up snapping and growling and biting on him some more and that wouldn't do either of them any good.

What she needed was to talk to somebody, get some unbiased advice on what she should do. That let out Mom and Pop. They'd do a dab dance if she told them, put on more pressure for her to say yes.

Nothing they'd like better than finally seeing her with a ring on her finger. Pop especially. Horace was the only man she'd ever been with whom he approved of, despite the hurt he'd put on her. And Pop had never approved of her work, not even when Bill made her a full and controlling partner in the agency. Thought it was the wrong kind of job for his daughter, too dangerous. Ridiculous. Man was a *cop,* for God's sake.

Claudia was out, too. They'd never gotten along. Polar opposites, her and her sister. Girl was a born-again and a vegan and, for all Tamara knew, still a virgin at thirty-three. She had an Oreo boyfriend, another lawyer like her, but they had separate apartments and there'd never been so much as a hint of them sleeping together. No plans to get married, either; Claudia was too independent, even more fiercely so than Tamara, to even consider giving up her freedom. That was another reason the folks would be thrilled with Horace's proposal — Tamara was their last best hope for a grandchild someday. Yeah, well, good luck with that. She was pretty sure the maternal gene had been left out of her. Horace said he didn't want kids, either, but he'd hedged by adding "at least not right away."

Bill? Kerry? No. No sense in burdening them with her personal problems; they had enough of their own to deal with. Besides, she felt bad about ragging on Bill on the phone Saturday for no good reason, just the crappy mood Horace and her period had put her in.

Vonda.

Sure, Vonda. They'd been friends since they were sophomores at Redwood High. Shared some wild times together in their gangsta/grunge days, chased with some bad-ass homies, smoked weed, done some things that came close to crossing the line. Vonda was slim and sleek with a J.Lo booty; guys had been all over her since she was fifteen. She must've done the nasty with fifty or so before she cleaned up her act. Which she'd done first the way Tamara had, by landing a good job as a sales rep at the S.F. Design Center, and then by falling for Ben Sherman, a stockbroker she met at a party. Their relationship seemed crazy in the beginning, loaded with problems, because Ben was both white and Jewish. They'd been married four years now, a real solid marriage from all indications. Who better to lend a sympathetic ear?

She called, and Vonda was home and free and willing to get together with her. They arranged to meet at a lounge near the Sherman apartment on Tel Hill.

"Well," Vonda said, "do you love the man?"

"Always have, you know that."

"Enough to want to spend the rest of your life with him?"

"I'm just not sure. That's the problem. We have a lot in common, as he keeps pointing out. Great sex, for one thing."

"Sex isn't enough, girlfriend."

"I know that, but —"

"Listen up." Vonda leaned forward across the table. It had been a while since Tamara had seen her; she looked as together and happy as ever since hooking up with Ben Sherman. "Truth is, Ben isn't the best lover I've ever had. I don't mean he's not good in bed; he is, just not the best. But he's kind and gentle and considerate, and he satisfies me every time. Because it's not just screwing; it's making love. Big difference."

Tamara wanted to say it was the same with Horace, making love instead of just humping, but she wasn't convinced it was. Instead she said, more defensively than she'd intended, "Horace is kind and gentle and considerate, too."

"I don't just mean in bed. I mean in everything you do together, day in, day out.

Ben and I hardly ever fight and when we do it's over and done with quick. We're like . . . well, sort of a black and white united front, know what I'm saying?"

"No trouble between you, no hassles."

"Right. None that matter. That's why our marriage works. I guess it's what makes any marriage work, when you come right down to it. What about you and Horace? Problems, hassles?"

"Not many since he came back from Philadelphia."

"Pretty heavy, the way he dumped you for that girl cello player."

"He's apologized dozens of times," Tamara said. "Swears he'll never be unfaithful to me again."

"You believe him?"

"I think he means it . . . now."

"But you're afraid you can't trust him in the future."

"Wouldn't you be?"

"This isn't about me. Have you forgiven him?"

"Well, mostly."

"But not a hundred percent."

"Hard to get all the way over what he did."

"For sure. Major question is, do you forgive him enough and trust him enough to marry him?"

". . . I'm just not sure."

Vonda took a sip of her white wine. "Why do you suppose he's putting so much pressure on you for an immediate answer?"

"He says it's time and he doesn't want to wait any longer."

"That's not much of an explanation."

"I know it."

"Look," Vonda said. "I'm gonna ask you something and I don't want you to take it the wrong way. Okay?"

"I won't. Go ahead."

"Could it be a money and security thing with him?"

Tamara said nothing, staring into her glass.

"So that's occurred to you, too, right?"

"Sure it has. But he's got a pretty good teaching job, he's making decent money at that and a little more playing chamber music —"

"And you've got a *very good* job and you're making, what, five or six times as much as he is. He'll never get another gig like he had with the Philadelphia symphony, will he?"

"Probably not."

"He must know it, too. He like teaching?"

"Says he does."

"Saying and meaning aren't the same

thing. A symphony cello seat is all he ever really wanted. And he's not getting any younger." Vonda tapped Tamara's hand gently with one of her pink-tipped nails. "I'm not saying he's looking to become a kept dude, or that he's got an eye on your income —"

"I'd scratch it out of his head if he did."

"— just saying that maybe the security thought's crossed his mind, too. Can't blame a man for thinking about his future."

"Or a woman for thinking about hers."

"Amen to that.

They were silent for a time. Vonda said finally, "So which way are you leaning, Tam? Yes or no?"

"God's honest truth? I don't think I'm ready for marriage. Not now, not yet."

"Then there's your answer, girlfriend. You've had it all along. Just needed me to get you to admit it to yourself."

Horace took her turndown well enough. No argument or anything, but it was plain that he was pretty damn disappointed. Because he really loved her and wanted to be with her? Because he'd miss the financial security she could give him? A combination of both?

Well, she'd find out. If they were still together a year, two years, from now and she was certain she could trust him completely again, and they developed the kind of tightly knit united front Vonda and Ben had in and out of bed, and he still wanted her to be his wife . . . maybe then she'd be ready and her answer would be yes.

20

JAKE RUNYON

He spent Sunday driving around the city, one end to the other, all the neighborhoods good and bad, stopping only to put gas in the Ford and twice to eat — once on Potrero Hill for a sandwich, the second time for dinner at a Chinese restaurant on Fillmore Street. Spending all or even part of the day at home in his Ortega Street apartment hadn't been an option. San Francisco was home now, but not the apartment. It was nothing more to him than a place for sleeping, watching TV when he needed a little downtime to recharge his batteries, doing computer research, and writing reports when necessary — he'd written up his report on the Dennison case Saturday night. A nowhere place, those four Spartan rooms; a lonely place.

Unless he was on a job, Sunday was the worst day of the week. A day when time seemed to slow to a crawl, a day to get through the best way he could. The only pleasurable Sundays since his move here from Seattle had been those he'd spent with Bryn — just the two of them at first and then, after she regained custody of her young son, Bobby, the three of them going places, doing things together.

He'd bonded with Bryn because of the stroke that had paralyzed the left side of her face, two damaged individuals leaning on each other for succor and support; bonded with Bobby, too, for a time, as though the boy were a surrogate son. But he'd felt all along that the relationships wouldn't last, and he'd been right; they hadn't. Bryn's whole life revolved around Bobby; once she had custody of him again and her ex-husband had come creeping back into the picture, she hadn't needed Runyon anymore and neither had the boy. Even though it was Runyon who'd been the catalyst responsible for the reconciliation of mother and son.

It had been six months now since he'd last seen either of them, the final meeting the day of Bobby's birthday when he'd stopped by their house to drop off a present for the boy. Bryn had berated him for coming by unexpectedly, the reason being that her ex was due soon to spend the day with her and Bobby. "Call before you come over next time," she'd said, and he'd said he would. But he'd known then there wouldn't be a next time. There'd been no contact of any kind between them since that day. Now the only time she entered his thoughts was on long, lonely Sundays.

This one finally ended and the new week began. He reported to the agency promptly at nine Monday morning. Tamara, as usual, was already at her computer. Her mood was good, upbeat, if a little on the quiet side; she seemed relieved about something, as if a weight had been removed, a problem solved. Good for her, if that was the case.

He'd e-mailed her the Dennison report, which she was in the process of reading when he came in. He supplemented it with a brief verbal summary, then asked if there was any new work for him.

"Nothing pressing," she said. "But I've got some news for you. Good news, maybe."

"I could use some. What is it?"

"Call last Thursday from your son Joshua."

Runyon was frankly astonished. "What did he want?"

"He wouldn't say. Just that he wanted to talk to you. I told him you were out of town on business."

"He didn't call me. No message on my cell or landline."

"Told me he'd lost your business card. I'd have given him your cell number, but he didn't identify himself until the end of the conversation."

"How come you didn't let me know right away?"

"He asked me not to. Said what he wanted to talk to you about could wait until today."

"He didn't give you any idea what it was?"

"No. None."

Runyon shook his head, an involuntary reaction. Three years, and no contact with Joshua in all that time. Why was he reaching out now, all of a sudden? Changed his mind about not wanting anything more to do with his father? That seemed too much to hope for. Wanted something again, probably, as he had the time his boyfriend, Kenneth, was assaulted by the pair of nightcrawlers. If that was it, it couldn't be too important if Joshua was willing to wait four days to discuss it.

Runyon went out to his desk in the outer office. Three years, he thought again. All that hate in Joshua's eyes the last time he'd seen him, even after all he'd done to put an end to the gay bashing. *I have all the reasons I need to hate you, twenty years and a dead mother worth of reasons.* The last words he had said to Runyon, making it clear that as far as he was concerned their estrangement was permanent, the rift between them irreparable.

But three years is a long time. Things happen; young men grow up and gain perspective and change their minds. Hope glimmering, only to be dashed again? Well, he told himself, don't speculate, find out.

Thirty-six months ago Joshua had been a trainee with a firm of financial planners at Embarcadero Center. Runyon looked up the number, called it, asked the woman who answered if he could speak to Joshua Fleming. Fleming — his mother's maiden name, legally changed to rid himself of Runyon's. The woman asked him to wait, left him hanging on hold for the better part of a minute. When she came back on she said, "I'm sorry, sir, Mr. Fleming is no longer employed here."

"When did he leave?"

"He was let go four months ago."

"Let go? You mean fired?"

"His position was eliminated."

Whatever the hell that meant. "Can you tell me where he's employed now?"

"No, sir. I have no idea."

It had been so long since he'd had a reason to call his son that he had to consult his address book for Joshua's home number. But when he tried it, he got a "We're sorry, this number is no longer in service" message.

He checked the city directory. No listing. Relied strictly on a cell phone, probably, like so many people these days. If he was registered with a provider company like AT&T, Tamara could track down the number. But if Joshua used one of the prepaid phones . . .

Moot issue. There was no need for any further checking because the agency's landline rang just then and Tamara answered and then came out to tell him that it was Joshua for him on line two.

Runyon picked up. "Hello, Son."

"Hello, Daddy dearest," in a half falsetto.

So that was how it was going to be. He should have known better than to hope for an olive branch. Or to expect common courtesy, for that matter.

"It's good to hear from you," he said.

"Is it? Never thought you would again, did you."

"I kept hoping, even when you wouldn't return my calls."

"Hope is the thing with feathers. That's a line from a poem by Emily Dickinson, in case you didn't know. It's also bullshit."

Runyon sidestepped that by saying, "I just tried to reach you at Hammond Smith Associates. I was sorry to hear you lost your job there. What happened?"

"They threw me out. Downsizing, they called it. More bullshit."

"Where are you employed now?"

"I'm not. No jobs for junior financial planners with my résumé."

"Sorry to hear that, too."

"Sure you are. Everybody I know is sorry. That's because most of them are sorry people."

"If I can help in any way . . ."

"Money? I don't want your money."

"Why did you get in touch after all this time, Joshua?"

"I want to see you."

"I'm glad to hear it. Why?"

"To talk. That's what you always wanted us to do, isn't it? Have a nice, long talk?"

"Yes. About anything specific?"

"Many things." Short, humorless laugh, almost a bark. "Shoes and ships and sealing wax, and cabbages and kings."

Runyon let that pass. There was a disturbing quality to Joshua's words, the pitch of his voice. Bitterness. Anger. And something else, a kind of disconnect, almost a wildness.

"Are you busy now?" Joshua said. "Can you come over to my place right away?"

"Sure I'll come. You're still at the flat on Hartford?"

"No. I had to move out of there. I'm living in an apartment on Dorland Street now. The Castro, same as always. Fag heaven."

"That was uncalled for," Runyon said gently. "You know I have no bias against homosexuality, yours or anyone else's."

"Oh, right, I forgot. I'll bet you're all for gay marriage, too."

"I'm all for people who love each other being together, yes."

"So am I. Not that it matters anymore."

"Are you still with Kenneth?"

"Christ, no. He's gone. Long, long gone."

"Someone new in your life?"

"That's one of the things we'll talk about when you get here, my love life. Sixty-four ninety-two Dorland, number two."

"I'll be there as soon as I can."

Joshua's former residence had been a large, ground-floor flat in a Stick Victorian on Hartford Street just off Twentieth. Good location, the Victorian in good repair. His current address on Dorland was a considerable come-down: one of half a dozen old, nondescript stucco buildings jammed together in the middle of the block, its façade and front steps cracked and paint-peeled. It housed four apartments, Joshua's on the ground floor rear.

Three of the mailboxes in the tiny foyer had names on them, one written on a piece of adhesive tape. The one marked #2 had no name at all. On purpose, Joshua living alone now and craving anonymity for some reason? Runyon pressed the bell button. Almost immediately a ratchety buzz released the lock on the security gate and he stepped through.

A short, dark hallway that smelled of Lysol led to the rear apartment. He knocked on the door.

From inside, somewhat muffled: "That you there, Jake Runyon?"

Not "Father" or "Dad": or even the pejorative "Daddy dearest." His full name, the way you'd address a stranger. Well, that was what they were and had been once Andrea got her poisonous claws into the boy, wasn't it? Strangers.

"Yes, it's me."

"The door's open. Come on in."

Runyon opened the door, stepped inside. He had a glancing impression of a living room unlike the neatly kept one in the Hartford flat, this one cluttered and untidy, but his attention was on his son. Joshua stood in front of a dark green armchair across the room, his body turned sideways. When Runyon shut the door, Joshua came all the way around to face him.

He had a gun in his hand.

And he pointed it straight at Runyon's belt buckle.

21

I was back on the Bay Bridge early Monday morning, just passing the Treasure Island exit, when my cell phone burbled. The call was from Walnut Creek police lieutenant Frank Kowalski.

"I rang up your office," he said after identifying himself, "and your secretary gave me your cell number."

"I don't have a secretary. Ms. Corbin is my partner. In fact, she's the agency's controlling partner."

"I see." He had a raspy voice, as if his vocal cords had been subjected to a sandpapering. Not a pleasant voice to have droning in your ear on the Bay Bridge. "I take it you know who I am?"

"The officer in charge of the Cahill murder case. My client's attorney, Moxon, gave me your name."

"Your client. Yes. I'd like to speak to you about your business arrangement with

James Cahill as soon as possible."

I wanted to say, *You are speaking to me,* but I didn't. I said, "Moxon told me that, too."

"Where are you now?"

"On the Bay Bridge, heading east."

"If you're thinking of trying to see Cahill, you're wasting your time. He isn't allowed visitors except for legal counsel until after his arraignment."

"I know. That's not where I'm going."

"To see me, then?"

"Eventually."

"Eventually?"

"I have some other things to do first."

"You're not still investigating on Cahill's behalf?"

"Would you object if I was?"

"Yes, I would," Kowalski said. There was an edge to the raspy voice now. "You know as well as I do that private detectives are not allowed to investigate a homicide."

"Unless they have police permission."

"Which you don't have and won't get. Did Cahill inform you he was under suspicion when he hired you?"

"Yes. He mentioned your name, as a matter of fact."

"Why didn't you inform me, then, that you'd been retained by him?"

"I wasn't obligated to at the time."

"You should have done so anyway."

I was in no mood for a lecture. Things on my mind, the little things I had told Kerry and Emily about yesterday, some of which I'd identified and pulled together — the main reason I was on my way to the East Bay again today. And I had woken up this morning with a sour stomach courtesy of Cellini's old-world spaghetti and meatballs and garlic bread and the glass of strong Chianti I'd drunk with the meal. Kowalski's officious attitude and raspy voice grated on me.

"A person under suspicion of a crime not yet established," I said, "has a legal right to hire a detective to work in his behalf, and the detective has a legal right to protect his client's interests as long as he doesn't break any laws or do anything to conflict or interfere with an official investigation."

He didn't like me quoting the law to him. "You're not going to give me any trouble, are you?"

"No. I always cooperate with the police — I was a cop myself once, for a lot of years."

"I've already checked on you," Kowalski said. "Do you have any knowledge germane to the murder investigation?"

It was not time yet to share my suspicions

264

with him, not until I had more information to back them up. I hedged by saying, "No specific knowledge, no. If I did, I would have given it to Moxon, and to you, right away."

A little satellite buzz on the line. Pretty soon he said, "I still want to see you. I'll be in my office most of the day until four. I'll expect to see you here before then."

"You will," I said. "One more thing for now, Lieutenant."

"Yes?"

"I'm still convinced James Cahill is innocent."

The first person I wanted to talk to was Fran Woodward, so I took Highway 80 off the bridge and then University Avenue into downtown Berkeley. But it turned out to be a wasted trip. She was out somewhere, evidently; no answer to my knock on the door to her studio or the front door of the house.

Grumbling a little to myself, I doubled back to 80 and then took 24 out through the Caldecott Tunnel to Walnut Creek and Shelter Hills Estates. Maybe it was my imagination, but the neighborhood seemed even quieter this morning than it had on my previous visit — the kind of hushed quiet that sometimes seems to settle on places where some kind of tragedy has happened. I parked in front of the Cahill house, crossed the street, and rang the bell at the house where Mrs. Cappicotti lived.

Spots, the Jack Russell terrier, set up a furious barking inside. I heard the lady tell him to "shut up, you," just before she opened the door. To my surprise, he obeyed.

She was wearing a bulky sweater and a pair of slacks today, both mint green. If she'd bothered to comb or brush her gray hair, she must have done it without benefit of a mirror; strands and wisps poked up in a half a dozen different places. Her lean face was solemn.

"Good morning, Mrs. Cappicotti. Remember me?"

"Sure. The detective. The police came and arrested Mr. Cahill on Saturday, but I guess you know about that. About poor Mrs. Cahill, too. It was on the local TV news last night." The terrier, hiding somewhere behind her, let out another bark. She told him again to shut up and again he obeyed. Then, to me, "Are you still working for Mr. Cahill?"

"Unofficially, yes."

"Well, I don't think he killed his wife. Naturally my daughter and her husband have the opposite opinion, seems like we

266

never agree on anything. You don't think he did it, do you?"

"No, ma'am, I don't."

"Ma'am. You're polite; I like that. There's too damn little civility in the world these days."

"I think so, too."

"What brought you back to see me? That car I had a glimpse of in the Cahills' garage?"

"Partially. I don't suppose you've remembered anything more about it?"

"Well, you know, I think I have. I've been thinking about it quite a bit and now I'm positive it was white, not beige or light tan or off-white. There's something else, too."

"Yes?"

"The taillights. I don't usually pay attention to how cars are designed these days — they all look pretty much the same to me except for their size — which is why I didn't remember this before now. I'm not absolutely sure, but I *think* I saw the taillights flash just before the door came down, and they were an odd shape. Not round like taillights used to be, but sort of oblong with the red parts in two *L*s, one on top of the other like neon strips. Does that make any sense?"

"Perfect sense."

"Does it help?"

"Yes, it does. Quite a bit."

"Well, good. I hope so."

"There's one more thing you can tell me, Mrs. Cappicotti. This may sound off the subject, but it's not and I have a good reason for asking. What time is the mail usually delivered here?"

"The mail?" To her credit she didn't ask what my good reason for asking was. "Between eleven-thirty and noon every day when our regular mailman, George Yamashita, is delivering."

"Would you recall if he was delivering the day Mrs. Cahill disappeared?"

"Well, he must've been," Mrs. Cappicotti said. "Every day except in the summer when he's on vacation. The relief people they put on then . . . phooey. Sometimes we don't get our mail until five o'clock. I can't imagine what takes them so long —"

I interrupted gently, "What sort of person is Mr. Yamashita? By that I mean is he friendly, willing to stop and talk?"

"Oh, sure. Very friendly, and polite like you. You want to ask him some questions, too?"

"Yes."

"Well, I'll be glad to introduce you, if you want."

"That might be a good idea."

"What time is it now? Ten-thirty?"

I looked at my watch. "Ten-forty."

"An hour or so. Would you like to come in and wait? Nobody home but me and the stupid dog. And there's a fresh pot of coffee on the stove."

Coffee was the last thing my innards needed right now. And as nice as Mrs. Cappicotti was, the last thing my head needed was an hour or more of idle chitchat.

I said, "Thanks, but there's something else I have to do. I'll be back by eleven-thirty."

"Okay, then. I'll keep an eye out for George in case he comes early."

I thanked her again, went over to the car, and drove to a nearby shopping mall that serviced the area. In a café next to one of the big-box stores I pampered my sour gut with milk and a jelly doughnut. At 11:15 I drove back to Shelter Hills and Sweet William Drive.

Mrs. Cappicotti was out front of her house, the terrier on his leash beside her. "No sign of George yet," she said when I joined her. She nodded at the dog. "I just finished taking him for a walk. Wouldn't poop at all today, would you, you annoying beast."

If I didn't know better, I could have sworn

Spots winked at her.

The wait for the mailman was less than ten minutes. Mrs. Cappicotti spotted his postal van first, in the next block. When the van crossed the intersection, she went over to the opposite side waving one hand and dragging the dog with the other, me at her heels. The van rolled to a stop in front of the Cahill house.

George Yamashita was in his fifties, slim and knobby kneed in a pair of regulation USPS shorts to go with his uniform jacket and cap. The sunny smile he favored us with said he was a man who enjoyed his work.

Mrs. Cappicotti performed the introductions. "He's a detective, George," she said. "He'd like to ask you a couple of questions."

"Questions?"

"About a delivery you made to the Cahills," I said, "on a Wednesday twelve days ago."

"Wednesday, twelve days ago. The day Mrs. Cahill disappeared?" He seemed not to know that her body had been found and her husband arrested. Mrs. Cappicotti had her mouth open to tell him, but I warned her off with a look and a headshake.

"That's right," I said. "You had a package addressed to her — books from her publisher in New York." I spread my hands to

270

illustrate the size.

He thought about it. "Oh, sure, I remember. Packages like that come for her now and then. Usually I ring the bell and she comes and gets them."

"But not that day."

"No. I rang the bell, but she didn't answer."

"So you left the package on the porch."

"She told me it was all right to do that. Sometimes she's too busy to come to the door."

"This is important, Mr. Yamashita. Was the red light on the security panel lit when you rang the bell?"

"The red light? Well, it always is when I bring the mail. I guess she feels safer with the security system on."

"But was it lit that day? Please try to remember."

I watched him working his memory again, frowning, shifting the bundle of mail he carried from one hand to the other. At length he said, "You know, now that you got me thinking, no, it wasn't."

"You're certain of that?"

"Yes, sir. I remember wondering how come she didn't have the system on as usual, but it wasn't any of my business so I just left the package and went on with my rounds."

I thanked him, and when he moved away Mrs. Cappicotti said, "What does it mean, the red light being off?"

"It means I'm on the right track."

"For proving Mr. Cahill didn't kill his wife?"

"Yes."

"Then you know who did?"

I said, "I can't say just yet," but the correct answer was yes.

22

Now I wanted more than ever to talk to Fran Woodward. In the car I looked up her cell number and called it. Four rings and I thought it was about to go to voice mail, but she answered on the fifth. I gave my name, asked if she was available to see me for a few minutes.

"I just now walked in the door," she said. "It's been a bitch of a morning and I need to take a shower and get some food. I haven't eaten all day."

"It's important, Ms. Woodward. A few more questions that won't take up much of your time."

"About the Cahills, I suppose."

"You know what happened on Friday and Saturday?"

"Kendra Nesbitt called to tell me the shitty news. I'm sorry Alice is dead, we were really close once, but I don't believe Jimmy killed her. He's a small-balls guy, like I told you before — just not capable of doing what the police claim he did."

"You're not alone in believing that."

"Good. Are you trying to prove it?"

"Working on it. That's why I need to talk to you."

"I don't know what I can tell you that I haven't already. But go ahead and ask your questions."

"They're better asked in person."

"Personal questions, then, I suppose. If you think I had anything to do with what happened to Alice —"

"No, I don't. A lot may depend on your answers, Ms. Woodward."

Pretty soon she said, "Where are you calling from?"

"Shelter Hills. I can be at your home in forty-five minutes or so."

"All right, then. I'll be in the house, not the studio."

It took me forty minutes because I parked close to her home, illegally, instead of wasting time driving around hunting a legal space. She took her time answering the door, a half-chewed sandwich in one hand. Turquoise streaks in her hair today, a somewhat different but no less jangly load of jewelry on fingers, wrists, ears, bare feet. Jeans and a pink sweatshirt with black lettering that read **FREE HUGS**.

"You drive fast," she said. "I haven't even finished my lunch."

"We can talk while you do."

She shrugged, led me into a kitchen decorated with half a dozen old-fashioned clocks and colorful art deco food posters that clashed with old yellow-flowered wallpaper that had begun to peel in places. A fat orange-and-white tomcat sat in the middle of a Formica-topped table, eyeing the remains of his owner's lunch.

"Get off the table, Garfield," she said. "You know you're not supposed to be up there."

The cat looked at her and yawned.

She shoved him off. "You're just like your namesake, you know that?" Then to me, "All I've got to drink is milk."

My stomach still hadn't settled. "Milk would be fine."

"Peanut butter sandwich to go with it?"

"Just the milk, thanks."

She got a carton out of the refrigerator, a glass for me, then poured some into a saucer for Garfield, who sniffed at it, gave her a disdainful look, turned his back, and sauntered out of the kitchen. I didn't blame him; the milk was fat-free. But what the hell, it was cold and relatively fresh.

275

"Okay," she said, taking a bite of her sandwich as she sat down, "so here we are. Ask away."

"I'm going to be blunt, Ms. Woodward. I think you weren't completely forthcoming with me the last time we talked."

"Is that right? What do you think I held back?"

"Information about Alice Cahill."

"Oh, really?"

"You told me she never spoke of the plagiarism accusation to you. Was that the truth?"

"Sure it was. Why?"

"Because the accusation was valid. She was a plagiarist. Possibly a multiple plagiarist."

"I don't believe it."

"It's true. The morning she was killed, she agreed to pay Grace Dellbrook two thousand dollars to avoid a scandal and a possible lawsuit."

". . . How do you know that?"

"Grace Dellbrook told me. Alice's e-mail to her proves it."

"Jesus."

"She did tell you about the accusation, didn't she."

Fran Woodward brushed bread crumbs off the front of her sweatshirt, wiped her hands on a dish towel. "All right, so what if she did? She's dead now; it doesn't matter anymore."

"It matters that she was a thief. Or didn't you care?"

"I cared; sure I cared. She said she only did it because she had a deadline to meet and she couldn't come up with an idea for another book of her own. She wanted my advice on what to do. I told her to own up, admit she'd made a stupid mistake, and pay the woman off."

"When was this?"

"The last time I saw her."

"And she agreed paying off was a good idea."

"Not then, she didn't. She threw one of her fits. Said suppose she did pay and the woman came back and demanded more money to keep quiet? She couldn't go on paying without Jimmy finding out."

"Obviously she changed her mind."

"Yeah, well, what other choice did she have? If the Dellbrook woman outed her to her publishers her career would be over, and what else did she have except her fucking writing?"

I didn't say anything.

"God, she was screwed up in so many

ways. The agoraphobia, the plagiarism, the —"

"The what? The reason she quit sleeping with her husband six months ago?"

Fran Woodward nibbled at a corner of her lower lip, rotated an etched copper bracelet on her left wrist, brushed again at the **FREE HUGS** emblem even though there weren't any more crumbs.

I said, "Come on, Ms. Woodward. You admitted that Alice told you they were no longer intimate."

"Yeah, she told me."

"And the reason why."

Another nibble, at the other lip corner this time. Then a tug at one of the dangly hoop earrings she wore.

"The last time I was here, you said she knew how to pleasure herself sexually. The implication was masturbation, but that wasn't what you meant. She had a lover."

"She couldn't leave the house —"

"She didn't have to leave the house. Her lover came there to see her as often as he could. The man you described as probably having 'a hell of a bedside manner.' The man who was once accused of sexual harassment by a woman who considers him a sexual predator. Dr. Paul Nesbitt."

"Oh, what the hell. Yes. She was having an

affair with Paul."

"He took advantage of her condition, seduced her —"

"Not exactly. She didn't say so, but I had the feeling she made the first move. She'd been attracted to him for a long time." Small, wry smile. "Best sex she'd ever had, she said. That's why she stopped sleeping with Jimmy. He'd never been able to satisfy her."

"He didn't have any idea what was going on?"

"Not a clue. Poor Jimmy. It would've hurt him bad if he knew."

"Her sister?"

"My God, no. As possessive as Kendra is, she'd have had a shit hemorrhage. Alice was very careful and so was Paul."

"How long have you known? From the beginning?"

"No, not until a couple of weeks ago. I think Alice kept it to herself for so long because she knew how I feel about Jimmy and she was afraid I'd let it slip to him or tell him outright. I wouldn't have and I didn't."

"Why did she confide in you then?"

"Paul wanted to break it off. Stop being her doctor, too. He thought they were getting too involved."

"And Alice didn't want the relationship to end."

"No. Paul wanting to walk out on her and the plagiarism thing had her climbing the walls. She'd started doubling up on her meds, but they weren't helping much."

"Anything else you think I should know about their relationship?"

"No. That's everything."

"I wish you'd been this frank with me the first time we talked, Ms. Woodward."

"I might have if I'd known Alice was dead and Jimmy was being blamed for it." Then, defensively, "I'm loyal to my friends, even when they're as screwed up as Alice was."

Loyal. Right. I said, "I'll be going now," and got to my feet.

"Wait a minute," she said. "What I just told you about Alice and Paul . . . you're not thinking he's the one who killed her?"

"Possible, isn't it?"

"Anything's possible. But I've known him for years. He's a doctor, he *saves* lives —"

"I'm just gathering information," I said, "not making accusations."

"Paul," she said, with awe in her voice. "If he did do it . . . Jesus. I guess you never really know anybody, do you."

No. You never do.

■ ■ ■ ■

Little things.

A long string of them, the few additional ones today confirming and cementing my suspicions. Added together, they pointed to one person and one person only.

The problem was that none of them, individually or collectively, constituted the kind of proof necessary to absolve James Cahill of guilt. Circumstantial evidence that might not even be enough to force an official investigation, much less an arrest.

I got the car going and started driving again. I had an idea, and so where I went was the one place I should not have gone.

23

JAKE RUNYON

Runyon went rigid, his arms and hands flat against his sides, his innards contracting as if yanked into knots by a drawstring. It wasn't just the gun or the unsteadiness of Joshua's hand; it was how he looked. Three years ago he had been a twenty-two-year-old pretty boy with Andrea's blond hair, blue eyes, narrow mouth, delicate features. He wasn't pretty now. He'd lost weight; his face was pale, drawn, unevenly stubbled, his long hair stringy, lusterless, uncombed and unwashed. Runyon's first thought was AIDS, the second hepatitis, the third cancer. Flashback memory of Colleen in the hospital bed, emaciated, wasting away, a shadow of her former self. He shoved free of it, quit thinking anything. Took a tight grip on himself.

"Why the gun, Joshua?"

"Don't try to come near me. Go over by

the window."

Runyon did that in slow, careful steps, his arms still pressed tight against his sides, his eyes on the gun. Small-caliber automatic, probably a five-shot .32. Not the most accurate of weapons except at close range, but deadly enough if the clip was emptied in rapid succession. The distance between them was about a dozen feet. He might survive a fast rush, given the unsteadiness of Joshua's hand and the probable fact that he'd had no training in the use of handguns. And he might not. It wasn't the way to handle this anyway, not even as a last resort.

Runyon asked again, "Why, Joshua?"

"Why do you think?"

"I don't know. You tell me."

"Oh, come on. You're a detective; figure it out."

"You hate me that much?"

"That much. Yes. You ruined my fucking life."

"Because of what you think I did to you and your mother."

"What I *know* you did to us."

"It's been three years," Runyon said. "Why decide to take me out now, after all that time?"

"Who says that's what I'm going to do?"

"What else is the gun for?"

Joshua laughed, an ugly sound with the edge of hysteria in it. His smoky blue eyes were very bright, unnaturally so. High on something to nerve himself up? Meth? One of the opioid narcotics? Hard to tell. The brightness could also be the result of an overload of anger and hatred, the kind of lethal mix that drives a person into temporary insanity.

"You don't want to do this," Runyon said. "Kill me and your life really will be ruined. You have no idea what prison is like."

"I'm not going to prison."

"You will if you pull that trigger. I'm not armed; you can't claim self-defense."

"They don't put dead men in prison, do they, Daddy dearest?"

The fingers of Runyon's right hand spasmed into a curl. Otherwise he didn't move, showed no reaction. "Murder/suicide, is that it?"

"That's what it was going to be. Not anymore." Abruptly Joshua lowered himself onto the old green armchair, sitting on the edge of a ripped cushion with his legs together, his right elbow propped on his knee, his left hand gripping his right wrist to hold the gun steady. "I'm not going to shoot you. Oh, no. I've got a better plan now."

"What plan?"

"Guess. Go ahead, guess."

"No."

"I'll give you a hint. Bang!"

"This isn't a game, Son."

"Don't call me that. I was never your son." The ugly little laugh again. He lifted the gun, turned it, placed the muzzle against his cheekbone. "This isn't for you, it's for me."

A frisson of coldness crawled up the back of Runyon's neck. "Shoot yourself in front of me, make me watch you die. Is that it?"

"That's it. Bingo. I knew you'd figure it out sooner or later, a great detective like you. Sherlock fucking Holmes."

"Willing to die just to make me suffer? Or is there more to it than that?"

"Oh, there's more. There's a lot more."

"Tell me what it is."

"Why should I? What do you care?"

"I care. I wish I could make you understand how much."

"Well, you can't. It doesn't matter anyway. Nothing matters anymore."

"Why don't you want to go on living?"

"Why. Why. The man I loved, *really* loved, walked out on me. I lost my job and I can't find another. I'm living in a shithole on unemployment insurance that's going to run out before long. And I have you for a father. What the hell do I have left to live for? Nothing."

Runyon let a few seconds pass before he spoke again. The tension in the room was charged; he could feel it as if parts of his body were attached to low-voltage electrodes.

"So you end your life and get back at me at the same time," he said then. "That seems right and fitting to you, does it?"

"Oh, it does. Bang! Two objectives accomplished with one shot."

"Would you do it in front of your mother?"

". . . What?"

"Kill yourself in front of her if she was still alive and I wasn't around to blame and punish?"

Violent headshake, setting the stringy blond hair aswirl; the automatic's muzzle made an audible scraping sound along his cheekbone. "Stupid goddamn question. I loved her, I hate you."

"She killed herself in front of you," Runyon said.

". . . What're you talking about?"

"Only she did it the slow way, day by day, with booze and hate. All the while feeding you steady doses of poisonous lies."

"Don't start that bullshit again —"

"It's not bullshit and you know it. Down deep you know it."

"Like hell I do —"

"She almost killed you quickly once, when you were a baby and we were still together. I told you about that three years ago, remember? The time I came home and found her in the bathtub, passed out drunk, holding you in her arms. You were asleep, your head barely above water. If she'd slipped down any further, you'd have drowned."

"Goddamn liar!"

"Postpartum depression and alcohol dependence. She started boozing in her teens, kept right on before and after we were married, and there wasn't anything I could do to help her."

"No! You never cared about her, never cared about me. You're the one who started her drinking by abandoning us — alcohol was the only way she could dull the pain."

"Listen to me, Joshua. Her father and mother were both alcoholics — her father died of cirrhosis, same as she did. She needed liquor to unwind, to be happy, to make love, to get through the day. I once offered to give you the names of people who could prove it to you. The offer still stands. But you don't really need proof, do you.

You lived with her nearly two decades — you know I'm telling the truth."

"Damn you, shut up!"

Sweat pimples spotted Joshua's forehead now. The automatic was once more pressed tight against his cheekbone, his finger in a convulsive back-and-forth slide across the trigger. Distract him — quick! There was a chair, a scarred ladderback, close to where Runyon stood; he went to it, moving neither fast nor slow, and sat down.

"What're you doing?"

"I felt like sitting. That's not a problem, is it?"

"No, it's not a problem. I don't give a shit." The laugh. "Front-row seat. It's almost time."

Runyon said slowly, "You think I don't know how you're feeling right now? The depression, the emptiness, the desire for oblivion?"

"You don't have a clue."

"Wrong. After Colleen died I was literally in the same place you are, sitting in a chair with a gun in my hand, working up to killing myself. I told you before that I watched her waste away with ovarian cancer. What I didn't tell you was that when she finally died I sat for three straight nights with the barrel of my service revolver in my mouth, sweating like you're sweating, trying to make myself eat a bullet."

"Why the hell didn't you?"

"I couldn't. Because Colleen wouldn't have wanted me to. Because I wasn't ready to die. Because I still had some things to live for. My work. You."

"Me? You never had me; you never wanted me."

"I tried to get custody of you after the divorce. I told you that before, too. But your mother had a smart lawyer, and she lied to the judge, made me out to be an abusive husband and father. He was an old-school disciplinarian; he believed her, read me the riot act, and gave her full custody. Right away she left Seattle and took you down here."

"You never once tried to visit me while I was growing up."

"Yes I did. The damn judge granted me visitation rights only at her discretion and my lawyer couldn't get the decision over-turned or modified. I tried half a dozen times to talk her into letting me see you, but she refused. I even flew down once unexpectedly when you were about six, but she wouldn't let me in, threatened to have me arrested if I tried."

"More bullshit."

"God's honest truth," Runyon said. "I gave up finally. I shouldn't have, and I'm sorry I did, but I'm not the kind of man who beats his head against a stone wall. I wish I was. I wish I had."

Joshua made a spitting mouth. "That's a lousy excuse."

"I'm not trying to excuse myself, I'm only telling you the way things were. I didn't think there was any hope, so I threw myself into my work. Long hours on the job, the longer the better. It was all I had until I met Colleen —"

"Colleen, Colleen."

"Yes, Colleen. A good woman, everything your mother wasn't."

"Don't start that crap again."

"All I had for twenty years, Colleen and my work," Runyon said, "but I never forgot you; I always intended to reach out to you once you were grown up, explain what really happened, try to regain your trust. If I'd known when your mother died, I would have tried then. But I didn't know until later. And Colleen was sick by the time I found out —"

"That's enough. Shut up! *Shut up!*"

Runyon shut up. The gun was pressed against Joshua's temple now, his finger no longer restlessly moving across the trigger.

Close to the edge, very close. In spite of what he'd said, he might not want to die as badly as he thought in his overwrought condition. But a trigger squeeze could just as easily be reflexive as voluntary. And silence only made the situation worse.

"Tell me about the man who hurt you, Joshua."

"What?"

"The man you loved so much, the man who left you."

"Why the hell should I? You don't care."

"I care that you were hurt by him. What's his name?"

". . . Brendon."

"How long were you together?"

"What difference does it make?" Joshua said. Then, "Fourteen months. The best fourteen months of my miserable life. I thought he loved me, but he was just another lying user like Kenneth."

"Why did he leave?"

"Why do you think? He found somebody else. Came home one night, threw it in my face, packed his stuff, and moved out. Fuck him. I don't want to talk about him."

This tactic wasn't going to work. It was only making Joshua more agitated, pushing him closer to the brink. Runyon had already discarded the idea of making an effort to disarm him; even standing, he would never make it across the room in time. What else? There had to be another way.

One, the only one he could think of that might work. Calculated high risk. But anything he said or did was a calculated high risk. He said a silent prayer, the first time he'd prayed since the early stages of Colleen's illness. Unanswered prayer then, shattering what little faith he had. If there was a God, He'd better be listening now.

Runyon sat still, very still, with his hands flat on his thighs. "Joshua," he said.

"What?"

"I'm as sick of this conversation as you are. If you're going to splatter your brains all over the room, go ahead and do it." The words burned in his throat; he had to force them out. "Get it over with."

"I will. You can't stop me."

"I'm not going to try anymore." He forced his eyes shut, squeezing the lids down tight. "But I won't watch you do it, I won't watch your head explode. And I won't look at what's left of you afterward. I'll just get up and walk out of here and call nine-one-one from outside."

"You don't mean that —"

"I *do* mean it. I won't give you the satisfaction."

"Open your eyes."

"No."

"Open your goddamn eyes!"

"Not until I hear the gun go off, and then only after I stand up and turn my back."

Silence again except for the rasp of Joshua's breathing. The only other times Runyon had felt this helpless were in the hospital at Colleen's bedside, and each of those times his eyes had been wide open. The strain of holding himself still quivered his nerves, set up a pounding ache in his temples. He could feel the accelerated beat of his pulse.

The crackling stillness seemed to go on and on and on. If the goddamn gun did go off, he didn't know what he'd do. Go a little crazy, probably.

But it didn't go off. There was a shift in the cadence of Joshua's breathing, a faint shuffling as if he was moving in the chair. And then a low moan that morphed into tremulous words.

"I can't. Oh God, *I can't!*"

Runyon counted to five, opened one eye to a slit. Joshua was bent forward in the chair, head tilted down so his chin touched his chest, the automatic no longer pressed to his temple; both elbows on his knees, the weapon held loosely in his upturned hand. His body began to shake. A keening sound burst out of him, then a spate of sobs — an intense release of long-trapped emotion. The gun slid from his fingers; he made no effort to stop it from falling. The thump it made hitting the threadbare carpet was like a benediction.

Prayer answered, this time.

Runyon exhaled the breath he'd been holding. Both eyes open now, he shoved to his feet, crossed the room quickly on the balls of his feet, bent to pick up the gun. The grip was slick with Joshua's sweat. He ejected the clip, dropped it into his coat pocket. There was a table a few feet away; he laid the empty automatic on it, came back to stand in front of the chair.

The sound of the heaving sobs was wrenching. The urge was strong in him to lean down and place a steadying arm around the hunched shoulders, say something calming, wipe away the tears, but he didn't give in to it. He stayed where he was, watching, listening, waiting.

Gradually the puling eased, ended in a series of shuddering breaths. After a few seconds Joshua lifted his tearstained face, looked up at him. In a broken half whisper he said, "What . . . what are you going to do? Beat me? Turn me over to the police?"

"Neither."

"What then?"

"Get you help. All the help you need."

"Why? Why would you do that, after what I tried to do to you?"

"Because I care what happens to you," Runyon said. "Because you're my son."

24

The idea I had was to see if I could manipulate Alice Cahill's murderer into making incriminating statements on tape. I keep a state-of-the-art voice-activated recorder in the car, one sensitive enough to pick up whispers even when tucked away inside a coat pocket. I've used it before, to good advantage. Such a recording is inadmissible in court, but if there's enough damning material contained on the tape it can be used to prod a perp into making a confession that *is* admissible.

I could have taken my collection of circumstantial evidence to Lieutenant Kowalski. It might have been enough to convince him to conduct an investigation, but I doubted it; he'd sounded pretty convinced on the phone that the guilty party was already in custody. Even if he gave my suspicions credence, he'd have had to admit he'd gotten them from me. And they'd have been angrily denied and likely to lead to a lawsuit for harassment. The one chance I had, or so I figured at the time, was the tape recorder ploy.

On the way to Lafayette, I worked out a series of questions and comments. Loaded ones, but none that could be construed as direct accusations. I had to be careful, very careful, in how I presented them.

The new cream-colored Lexus was parked where it had been on my last visit, in the long curving driveway. All right, good, Kendra Nesbitt was home. Now, if she was alone, all I had to do was talk my way inside.

I parked a short distance beyond the driveway, transferred the recorder from the glove compartment to my coat pocket. Locked the car, even though nobody was likely to bother it in a neighborhood like this, and trudged back to the Nesbitt property and up the drive to the front porch.

Some sort of chimes echoed inside when I pushed the bell. There was no one-way peephole in the door, just a fancy-colored fanlight that you could probably look through from inside if you stood up on your toes. Kendra Nesbitt didn't do that. There was no chain on the door, either; a click and she opened right up.

Casually and immaculately dressed today

in a caramel-colored blouse and black slacks. Short dark hair neatly combed. Rouge on her cheeks, mouth painted with the bright red lipstick she preferred. And a tight-lipped scowl when she recognized me.

"You again," she said. "I told you not to bother me anymore."

She would have shut the door in my face, except that I got a foot in the way and then a shoulder block. "I think you'd better talk to me, Mrs. Nesbitt."

"Why should I? I have nothing more to say to you."

"But I have some things to say to you."

"What things?"

"About your sister's murder."

"James is in jail, in case you don't already know it —"

"I know he is, yes. I also know he didn't kill her."

She tried again to shut the door, banging it hard against my foot and shoulder. When I didn't back off, she snapped, "Do you want me to call the police and have you arrested for trespassing?"

"That's your right," I said, "but it won't change the situation any."

"What situation? What're you talking about?"

"I have information that I believe exonerates James Cahill, points the finger elsewhere."

Her control was good. Flicker of emotion in the brown eyes, a faint muscle twitch alongside the red-painted mouth. "What information?"

"Suppose we talk inside. Or if you're not alone, step out and we'll talk here on the porch."

"I don't want you in my house." She said it defiantly.

"I'm no threat to you, Mrs. Nesbitt. At least not physically."

". . . What is that supposed to mean?"

"Inside or outside, your choice."

I watched her struggle with it. Put on a hard, narrow-eyed look to help her make up her mind. Concern that I did know something harmful to her won out. She said in glacial tones, "I'll give you ten minutes," and pulled the door inward.

I had my hand in my coat pocket as I stepped over the threshold. Now that the preliminary push was over and I was inside, I flipped on the recorder as I followed her.

Where she took me was into a formal living room off the vestibule. Lush pale blue carpeting, chintz curtains, modern rose-patterned couch and chairs, a kidney-shaped coffee table with a large blue-and-white vase in the middle of it. She went over by a blond-wood sideboard, stood facing me with arms folded across her heavy breasts. I stopped at the end of the couch, the coffee table between us.

"Well?" she said.

I said, "The day your sister disappeared, the day she was killed. You went to see her that morning about ten, to bring her a new prescription of Valium."

She didn't say anything.

"You told me previously that she and her husband had an argument before he left for work, that she was upset when you got there. Very upset. Is that right?"

"Yes, so?"

"Then why didn't she take one or more of the Valium?"

". . . What?"

"According to you, and to her husband, she'd run out. That's why you brought her the new bottle. But it was never opened. How come, if she was so agitated?"

Caught her off guard, but not for long. "Alice hadn't run out completely, only thought she had. She'd found a few in her bathroom drawer, taken two just before I got there. They take a while to work, you know."

A lie, but a plausible one, dammit.

300

"How long did you stay with her?" I asked.

"Not long, if it matters. Until she calmed down."

"Half an hour, longer?"

"I didn't look at my watch."

"Why didn't she switch on the security alarm after you left?"

"She did. She always did."

"So I've been told. Part of her phobia. But she didn't that morning."

"How do you know she didn't?"

"The mailman came by around eleven-forty-five with a package of books for her. He rang the bell, but she didn't answer, so he left the package on the porch. I talked to him earlier today. He remembers that the red light on the porch panel was turned off."

"How can he be sure of that after nearly two weeks? His memory must be faulty."

"He remembers it clearly because the light was always on whenever he had a delivery for her. Every time. Except that day. Why didn't your sister arm the system after you left?"

"How should I know? She was agitated; she may have gotten distracted and forgotten."

"She never forgot before."

"You don't know that. You didn't know Alice."

So far this was not working out as I'd hoped. And the room was overheated; she must have had the furnace turned up over seventy even though it was a clear, warmish spring day. I would have liked to shed my coat, but I did not want to take the chance with the recorder going in the pocket.

I said, "The woman who lives across the street, Mrs. Cappicotti, saw a car going into the Cahills' garage around one o'clock —"

"*Thought* she saw a car. She's old and her eyesight isn't very good."

"A white car with distinctive taillights, two red L-shaped strips. That identifies it as a new Lexus."

"And I suppose you think it was mine she thought she saw. Well, it wasn't. Thousands of people drive Lexus cars."

"You didn't go back to the Cahills' that afternoon?"

"No. I had no reason to."

"Where were you at one o'clock?"

"I don't have to answer that, but I will. Nowhere near Shelter Hills. Out to lunch with a friend, if you must know."

A good friend willing to lie for her, I thought. But I couldn't say it because it constituted an accusation.

"If the Cappicotti woman did see a car," she said, "it was Jim's."

"He doesn't drive a Lexus."

"I told you, her eyesight is poor. And *he* doesn't have an alibi for one o'clock. Besides, he's the only one who could have opened the garage door."

"Not so," I said. "There was a spare opener in a drawer in the kitchen. It's gone now."

"Well, I never saw it. You think I poke around in kitchen drawers? Besides, you only have his word there was a spare."

"If your sister was still alive at one o'clock, why would he have driven into the garage instead of parking in the driveway or on the street?"

"How should I know? Maybe he didn't kill Alice in a sudden rage; maybe he intended to murder her all along."

"With a laptop computer? Pretty unusual murder weapon."

No reaction to that. This wasn't going well at all. And I was sweating now inside the damn coat.

"And after she was dead," I said, "he allegedly wrapped up her body without removing her wedding ring and including the laptop, then put her in his car, drove her way over past Martinez, and dumped her more or less in plain sight."

"He panicked. That's what the police think."

"Or the person who actually killed her wanted her to be found and identified so he'd be blamed. And when she wasn't found right away, that person made the anonymous phone call to the police."

"Oh, crap. What are you trying to say? That *I'm* that person?"

"Are you?"

"No! What reason would I have for killing my own sister?"

"She was having an affair with your husband."

Kendra Nesbitt's arms unfolded, her hands closed into fists; the dark eyes bulged. She stood as stiff as block of wood. Her mouth barely moved when she said in a low, savage voice, "You son of a bitch. Who told you that?"

"Fran Woodward."

"It's a goddamn lie."

"She has no reason to lie. Did you know about the affair, Mrs. Nesbitt?"

"There was no affair." She jabbed a fist in my direction, a movement like a hammer pounding a nail. "I don't have to listen to any more of these ridiculous accusations."

"I haven't made any accusations —"

"I won't stand for it, not from you, not

304

from Fran, not from anybody." Cold anger, as cold and sharp as a blade of ice.

I could have gone on with it. Confronted her with the rest of the little things: the plagiarism business, the telling comment she'd made to me on my first visit about goddamn cheating men, the lies about Cahill's excessive drinking and aggressive attitude toward his wife, the red herring mention of the one-hundred-thousand-dollar life insurance policy. But what good would it do? She hadn't cracked on any of the other points; she wouldn't crack on those, either. She was clever and she had a quick mind; she hadn't said much of anything at all to incriminate herself. Bad idea coming here. Foolish. Loss of perspective, neglect of proper procedure.

"Your ten minutes are up," she said. "Get out of my house and don't ever come back."

The sourness in my gut kicked gas up into my throat. I couldn't quite suppress the belch in time.

"You're disgusting," she said. "If you don't leave right now, I will call the police."

"Look, Mrs. Nesbitt —"

"I won't tell you again. Get . . . out . . . of . . . my . . . house."

"All right. With pleasure, lady."

She took a step toward me, and I backed

up one in reflex, and all at once I felt dizzy. And then nauseous. And my left shoulder had begun to ache. I retreated another step, faltering, reaching out to the back of the couch with my right hand to steady myself. I tried to lift my left arm to flex it, and a lancet of pain shot all the way down to my fingertips.

Sudden fear surged through me — justified, because the next eruption of pain was excruciating, as if I'd been kicked in the chest. The force of it took my breath away.

It must have knocked me down. I don't remember falling, but there were crashing sounds, a yell from Kendra Nesbitt . . . and I was on my ass on the floor, my body bent so that I was half-sitting with my head and shoulders against the side of the couch. I could not get enough air into my lungs, heard myself making little gasping sounds.

"You clumsy oaf! Look what you did to my antique delft vase!"

I could neither hear nor see clearly; there was a dull thrumming in my ears, a thin gray fuzz clouding my vision. Through the grayness I could make out the coffee table lying on its side, shattered pieces of the glass bowl that had been on it. I tried to lift myself up, but I had no strength; it was as if heavy weights had been attached to my arms or legs. The fear ripped at me again.

The woman's white face came swimming out of the mist. I heard her say through the thrumming, "What's the matter with you?"

". . . Pain . . . chest, left arm . . ." I could barely get the words out.

"Sharp, dull, crushing?"

". . . Like a hand . . . squeezing . . ."

"Hard to breathe?"

". . . Yes."

"Can you move, get up?"

I tried again. I might as well have been trying to lift a thousand-pound stone.

"Cardiac arrest. Heart attack."

Oh, God, no, not now, not here!

Fingers groped at my wrist. "Rapid pulse." Very calm now, the voice still cold but without the sharpness, matter-of-fact. "Skin all gray and dripping sweat, squeezing pain, difficulty breathing, unable to move. Severe coronary. Very severe."

". . . Call nine . . . one. . . ."

"The kind that will surely kill you if you don't get immediate treatment."

"Nine . . . one . . . one . . ."

"My husband taught me what to do in a case like this. I should make you lie flat on your back, knees up, then cover you with a blanket to keep you warm. Give you baby aspirin. Call the emergency number and

307

perform CPR if your heart stops beating before the paramedics come."

". . . Please . . ."

"But I don't think I'll do any of that. Why should I, after all your snooping? You're a threat to my safety. I think I'll just let you die."

No! Again I tried to lift myself; again I could do nothing except jerk and twitch spasmodically. The squeezing pressure in my chest seemed to be intensifying. Fuzziness in my head now so that I could no longer think clearly. A feeling of black despair moving through me.

The white face went away. Faint squeak of couch springs audible through the thrumming as she sat down nearby. Then her voice again, as if from an even greater distance.

"Can you still hear me?"

I seemed to have lost the power of speech. All I could do was make grunting, choking sounds.

Louder: "Serves you right, coming into my house, accusing me, then having your goddamn heart attack in my living room. But now that it's happened I'm glad you came. You're the only one who suspects the truth, the only one who can give the police cause to change their minds. Even if by some miracle you were to survive, it would be your word against mine that I didn't try to save you. I'd just say you were delirious from the pain, I did everything I could. But that won't happen, the miracle I mean. Those sounds you're making — it's getting harder and harder to breathe, isn't it? It won't be much longer now. I'll just sit here and wait; I don't have to do anything else. Or anything else to do."

"Unh. Unh."

"Should I put some music on? Let's see, what would be appropriate? How about something classical? Chopin's 'Funeral March'?"

Crazy woman . . . psychotic . . .

"No? All right, then, suppose I amuse myself by telling you what you want to know. Yes, I killed Alice. I didn't intend to when I went there. It was her fault, not mine. All her fault. Damn her, she deserved what she got for what she did to me."

". . . Unh . . ."

"She was in one of her miserable bitchy moods that morning because she'd had another e-mail from the Dellbrook woman, threatening a lawsuit, and she was going to pay her two thousand dollars to keep her quiet. She was so upset, she let it slip out — that's how I found out she was a plagiarist. And it wasn't just one theft; oh no, there were others, too, because her publishers wanted more and more books and she couldn't come up with enough ideas of her own. Can you imagine how I felt? My own sister, a thief on top of everything else. It made me furious and we started arguing; we were always arguing. It got so heated she completely lost control and started screaming at me that she'd been fucking my husband for the past six months. Six months! Once a week, twice a week, every chance she had. Well, I lost it, too. I slapped her and she tried to claw me and I had to defend myself, didn't I? We were in her office and I picked up her laptop without even thinking and hit her with it, twice, and then she was dead."

". . . Unh . . . unh . . ."

"I suppose I should have been sorry, but I wasn't. Agoraphobe, thief, husband stealer . . . bitch! I left her there on the floor and went home. At first I thought it was the right thing to do because James was sure to be blamed. But Alice was alive when he left for work; she'd called Paul to tell him she was out of Valium. And I remembered about autopsies being able to determine when a person died. James left the house more than three hours before I killed her; she hardly ever let strangers in, and I was her only visitor that morning. The police were sure to find out I'd done it unless her body wasn't found there in the house.

"So I went back there and got the spare garage door opener from the kitchen and then put my car in the garage. No one saw me except that damned busybody across the street. There wasn't much blood, I cleaned up what there was. Then I put Alice and the computer in garbage sacks and tied up the bundle with duct tape and carried her out to the car and put her in the trunk. It wasn't difficult, I'm strong and she didn't weigh very much. I wasn't sure where to take her. Someplace where she'd be found fairly soon and James would be blamed. Then I remembered the Waterbird preserve, Paul and I went there once years ago. When I got there I found what seemed to be the perfect place, made sure I was alone, and shoved her down into that little gully. It was a big risk, doing all of that, but I've never been afraid to take risks. You do what you have to do. Like now, with you."

". . . Unh . . ."

"But nobody found her. I couldn't believe it. Days went by . . . couldn't stand the waiting any longer so . . . matters into my own hands again and called the sheriff's department . . . one of those disposable phones so

311

the call couldn't be traced. . . ."

Her voice fading, the buzzing in my ears louder so that I heard only snatches of what she was saying.

". . . James deserves to be blamed . . . screwing that Sprague woman . . . saw them with their heads together in a restaurant, her hand on his . . . knew right away what was going on . . . trying to do what was best for Alice and all the time she and Paul . . . he's mine; she had no right . . . thief, husband stealer, my own sister. . . ."

I could no longer hear her. Stopped talking? The gray mist had darkened so that I could barely see anything in the room. The pressure in my chest was intense now, pain radiating up and down my left arm. Another surge of fear. Random thought: What a lousy way to die.

I heard something else then, far off, a faint banging sound. Followed by another voice calling her name.

Help!

She was talking again, the other voice, too, far away at first and then coming closer so that I was aware of some of the words from both, jumbled together into disjointed fragments.

". . . doing home this early, didn't expect you until . . . heart attack . . . when . . . just now . . . where is he . . . there in the living room . . . just about to call . . . too late. . . ."

Then her voice again, the last thing I heard before the gray dissolved into black, saying as if she were whispering the words into my ear, "He's dying. I think he's almost dead."

25

Kendra Nesbitt came close, very close, to being right.

Whatever else you could say about her husband, he was a competent physician and good in a crisis. Dr. Paul Nesbitt literally saved my life.

If he hadn't come home when he did — Monday was his surgery day; he'd been up since 4:00 A.M. and had performed a difficult operation that lasted several hours; he was tired and in need of some R & R — and if he hadn't acted quickly and efficiently I would have died on his living room floor. As it was, he told his wife to call 911 — she couldn't very well refuse — while he got me stabilized, administered baby aspirin and nitroglycerin pills to make the platelets in the damaged heart artery less sticky, minimize the threat of blood clot formation, and prevent further blockage. The EMTs got there in eleven minutes; they put me on a cannula of oxygen and hauled me off to the Walnut Creek branch of the John Muir Medical Center.

Touch-and-go there, too. The ER doctors administered clot-busting medicine, did whatever else they do to further stabilize heart attack victims, then put me in ICU. X-rays indicated the necessity for a nonsurgical procedure called coronary angioplasty to open two blocked arteries in the heart, and this was administered.

The first few hours are critical; make it through them and your survival rate rises exponentially, the more so when you're blessed with the strong support of loved ones. When I first woke up in ICU, Kerry was there holding my hand, telling me she loved me, saying, "You're not going to leave us, I need you, Emily needs you, you're going to be fine" — her touch and her words giving me hope, strength, courage.

Emily was with her the second time she came, later that same day. She kissed my cheek, fighting back tears, and whispered, "Get well, Dad. Please, please. I love you so much." More urgent support for me to hang on to.

The damage I'd suffered was extensive. Diagnosis: open-heart surgery. Once they considered me strong enough, I underwent a coronary artery bypass. Translation: a healthy artery is removed from another part of the body, in my case the inner thigh, and then grafted to bypass the blocked section of the damaged artery so as to provide a new route for blood to flow to the heart muscle. Dr. Nesbitt did not perform the surgery; he hadn't administered the coronary angioplasty, either. Both were done by a well-regarded Indian cardiologist named Abhay Rajneesh.

The operation was deemed a success.

I was in the hospital for six more days. Kerry was there at my bedside every day, bringing Emily with her three more times. Tamara and Jake Runyon each visited twice. Lieutenant Frank Kowalski, who despite his raspy voice looked more like a clergyman than a cop, also came twice. I had a few other visitors, too. Mrs. Cappicotti, of all people. And James Cahill and Megan Sprague together. Plus I had phone calls from a couple of longtime corporate clients and an old poker buddy, Jack Logan. Nice to know people care when you're down and close to having been out.

Cahill represented the one good thing that came from my near-death experience. Dr. Nesbitt had not found the voice-activated recorder pocket when he took off my coat;

neither, thankfully, had his wife. I asked about it when I was well enough to consider such things, and it turned out the coat had gone to the hospital along with me in the ambulance. Somebody in the ER (I never did get the person's name) had found it and put it away for safekeeping with my other possessions. I told Kerry about it, and she retrieved it and played the tape and then gave the recorder to Tamara, who turned it over to Lieutenant Kowalski.

The dialogue exchange and Kendra Nesbitt's impromptu confession were on there as clear as could be — my ineffectual attempts to incriminate her, every word of her intent to let me die, her confession of the murder of her sister. Kowalski's first visit to the hospital was to get the rest of my story before he went after her. At first, out of desperation, she tried to claim the tape was false, the voice on it wasn't hers, one of my "people" must have manufactured it. Kowalski didn't buy any of that, of course. He broke her down finally, and she made a formal confession, and that let James Cahill off the hook and earned him his freedom.

So I'd done the wrong thing by going to the Nesbitt home, yet I'd also inadvertently and ironically done the right thing. But I'd paid a hard price. I did not realize just how hard — or maybe I did, just refused to consider it — until Dr. Rajneesh and I had a long talk shortly before I was released.

Even with the bypass surgery, my heart was in a weakened condition. The reasons were all too obvious in retrospect. Too much physically and mentally induced strain over most of my adult life. Chronic high blood pressure. Ill-advised eating habits and insufficient weight control. Failure to have regular medical checkups.

Five to six weeks of complete rest at home were indicated to begin with. In addition to having to take ACE inhibitors to lower my blood pressure and prevent further weakening of the heart muscle, I needed to change my diet, lose the few pounds of excess weight I carried and keep them off, learn to manage stress (his recommendation was a program of relaxation therapy), and reduce physical activity. Stabilizing blood pressure and managing stress were particularly important, he said. Even though I only worked an average of two days per week, I was nonetheless engaged in a high-stress profession, as the circumstances leading up to my heart attack proved. If I wished to avoid another, perhaps fatal coronary and live a long and healthy life, his recommendation was that I remove myself entirely from this taxing environment.

In other words, pack it in. Fully retire.

I talked it over with Kerry, of course. She was all for it. "I don't want to lose you," she said. "Emily doesn't want to lose you."

"What would I do with myself?" I said. "Rattle around the condo all day, stare at the TV? Take up cooking or some other hobby I have no real interest in? Vegetate? You can only do so much reading, listen to so much music."

"That's a weak argument and you know it. There are plenty of things you can do. Non-stressful volunteer work. Consult. Teach. And we've always wanted to travel, haven't we?"

"You're still working full-time, you can't take the time off to travel."

"Yes I can. And I will. We're financially secure. We can afford to go anywhere we want to, whenever we want to."

I talked it over with Tamara, too. Same results. She was perfectly capable of running the agency on her own; she pretty much did so now as it was. Simple enough to bring in another operative to handle the work I'd been doing. She would need to consult with me from time, no doubt, but I could accommodate her on the phone without undue stress. My health was the most important thing. Nothing else mattered.

That was what it all came down to, the health issue. Kerry did not want to lose me, Emily did not want to lose me, Tamara did not want to lose me. And I did not want to lose myself.

Still, I struggled a little with the decision. Just a little, and not for long. Hell, it was time, not only because of the coronary but also because of the way I'd mishandled the final stage of the Cahill investigation — the inevitable slow erosion of skills wrought by age. I knew it, accepted it. So the day I came home I made it official. Endgame. In a way it was a relief, because from now on I would be free of situations that bred tension and turmoil, no longer need to fire a gun even on a practice range, no longer have to deal with shattered lives, no longer be plagued by ghosts.

Regrets? None worth mentioning.

It was a hell of a ride while it lasted.

ABOUT THE AUTHOR

Bill Pronzini has been nominated for, or won, every prize offered to crime fiction writers, including the Grand Master Award from the Mystery Writers of America. It is no wonder, then, that *Detroit Free Press* said of him, "It's always nice to see masters at work. Pronzini's clear style seamlessly weaves [storylines] together, turning them into a quick, compelling read." He lives and writes in California, with his wife, crime novelist Marcia Muller.

The employees of Thorndike Press hope you have enjoyed this Large Print book. All our Thorndike, Wheeler, and Kennebec Large Print titles are designed for easy reading, and all our books are made to last. Other Thorndike Press Large Print books are available at your library, through selected bookstores, or directly from us.

For information about titles, please call:
  (800) 223-1244

or visit our website at:
  gale.com/thorndike

To share your comments, please write:
  Publisher
  Thorndike Press
  10 Water St., Suite 310
  Waterville, ME 04901